Galvanized Yankee

From the bloodstained fields of the Civil War, through a brutal Indian campaign and finally into the greedy, lawless world of the Montana goldfields, Jared Harris is relentlessly pursued by mysterious enemies. Who are they, what do they want and why him?

Now he finds himself accused of a murder he did not commit, hunted by hooded vigilantes and, worse still, pursued by the Army for dereliction of duty. Time is running out for Harris and, if he is to find the key to his survival, he must face the man who plunged him into this unending nightmare.

But will he survive the gamble?

Galvanized Yankee

MARK BANNERMAN

A Black Horse Western

ROBERT HALE · LONDON

ISBN 0 7090 6870 0

Robert Hale Limited
Clerkenwell House
Clerkenwell Green
London EC1R 0HT

Typeset by
Derek Doyle & Associates, Liverpool.
Printed and bound in Great Britain by
Antony Rowe Limited, Wiltshire

For
Will Henry, Ernest Haycox, Jack Schaefer
and all the other great Western writers
who have been my inspiration

ONE

Jared Harris travelled through the mountains on the Umatilla stage and reached Idaho City, in the Boise Basin, at noon on a torrid June day of 1872. He dismounted in dusty Main Street close to the new courthouse and stretched the kinks from his arms and legs. Everywhere was bustling despite the heat; the discovery of gold in nearby Grimes and Elk Creeks had ensured that the town changed from a quiet backwater, undisturbed by the Civil War, into a thriving centre that had attracted prospectors in thousands, and with them the inevitable merchants, gamblers, confidence men, petty thieves and prostitutes.

Today, a line of wagons stood in the street and men were loading sacks of flour for conveyance to the mines, and, further along, a quack doctor was peddling his bottled wares, his boasts rising above the babble of voices.

Harris was a lean Kentuckian whose harrowing past had left deep-drawn lines on his face, a wariness to his manner, and a mien beyond his thirty years. He chose not to speak more often than was necessary for

7

he had found that his Southern drawl still aroused resentment amongst Northerners. He was wearing a slouch hat with the brim pulled low, a faded suit which had seen better days and was creased from the jolting ride aboard the stage, and a pair of army boots.

Right now, he could feel the familiar tightening in his chest, the rising up of old fears, and he knew that he was taking the gravest risk in coming here. He touched the .44 calibre Navy Colt in his waistband, inwardly praying that this day would not bring the necessity for gunplay, yet he knew there were scores to settle and he was dealing with a man whose mind might be twisted beyond reason. But Jared Harris would find no peace until he had faced James Shafter and, one way or another, resolved the madness which had hounded him these past years.

He had an idea that Shafter owned a house on the north side of town, but he had not been to Idaho City before and he would need to inquire for directions. But firstly he felt in need of fortifying, so he stepped as inconspicuously as possible into the busy ambience of a saloon. The place was packed with a cosmopolitan throng of men and not a few fancy-dressed women, the clink of glassware competing with their voices and the jangle of a nickelodeon. Several poker games were in progress and, at one end of the bar, a man had a rattlesnake in a large jar and was taking bets as to who could stare into the reptile's eyes and not flinch as it made its dart.

Jared eased his way to the bar, acquired whiskey and a glass and found himself a vacant chair in the far corner of the room. He was a man who could not exist

with a challenge unmet, and right now he hoped he
was on the threshold of bringing some meaning to his
wasted years. Images of those who had died flitted
through his mind, battlefields carpeted with corpses,
the blood-soaked blue and grey of their uniforms no
longer of consequence. He saw eyes widened in death,
and the cries of the wounded forever haunted him. He
saw men crippled, arms or legs cut off by surgeons
whose only recourse, in those gory field hospitals, was
amputation. And he saw the face of his dear wife,
Annie, smiling bravely, her eyes bright and her lips
whispering how she longed for the day when they
would be reunited. Now, such a day would never come,
not this side of Heaven.

He tried to focus his attention on what lay ahead.
James Shafter . . . he had travelled a thousand miles to
find him. This was the man who had ruined his life, yet
his mission was not one of vengeance. Instead his great
desire was to lay to rest what he believed was a horrendous misunderstanding. He prayed that somewhere in
James Shafter's heart there might reside a shared
wish. He drained his glass, knowing that the matter
could be delayed no longer.

He checked his Navy Colt once more, reassuring
himself that it was loaded and that it would slip from
his waistband without impediment. He left the saloon,
and on the boardwalk inquired of a storekeeper if he
knew James Shafter and, if he did, where he lived. His
question sparked off an immediate reaction.

'Sure I know Major Shafter. He lives in one of them
fine houses on the creek, north side of town. The place
has a sign up saying SHAFTER'S HALT. You can't miss it.'

He eyed Harris up and down and then went on; 'I'd sure watch out if I was you, mister. Shafter is a sick man and as dangerous as hell. He was involved in some fight with the Indians a few years back, and he keeps reliving the battle. I heard he paces around his room, dressed up in his uniform, imagining he's surrounded by red varmints. He keeps firing off his revolver. There's so many bullet-holes in his ceiling, the rain comes in. He drives his sister Ella to distraction.'

Following the man's directions, Harris left the main thoroughfare, finding the quiet trail that wound northward through wooded land until he reached a cleared stretch, alongside a creek. Here stood some fine houses, obviously built before the Boise Basin had become exploited by man's greed for gold. This was a place that contrasted starkly with the crude scramble of Main Street.

The houses, standing well apart in fenced meadows, were of white-painted timber, and had three-storeys with decorous pillars, balconies and porches. Jared had always suspected that Shafter came from a moneyed family and now this seemed confirmed. He soon saw the finger-board proclaiming SHAFTER'S HALT, stepped through the front gateway, walked across the meadow and climbed wide steps to the door. He raised his hand to the Caesar's Head knocker and heard its resonance echo through the hallway inside. He waited, conscious of his heart pounding against his ribs, then he heard the brisk step of a woman, and the door was drawn open. He touched the brim of his hat, but there his hand paused. The face that confronted him possessed the same eyes as those of the man he sought, the same wide mouth – and yet, strangely, she was not unpretty. Her light-brown hair was drawn into a chignon and she was slim and wore a pink calico dress, decorated with neatly pressed ruffles. His mind raced, reached the conclusion that this was the man's sister, Ella. He thought maybe she was thirty-five.

'I've come to see James Shafter,' he said.

A look of alarm passed across her face, her blue eyes widened, then softened.

'Who are you?' she asked.

'I'm Jared Harris, an old ... acquaintance ... of Major Shafter.'

'Your voice is Southern,' she said. 'You must have been an enemy of his.'

'I served alongside him in the Frontier Army. I was what they call a Galvanized Yankee.'

She nodded, but she was still uncertain. 'He has not been well. His mind is full of what happened to him. He does not live in the present, only the past. He may not be very hospitable towards you.'

'I understand that,' Jared said, 'but there are matters that must be sorted out. Perhaps he will find peace of mind once we have spoken, and me too.'

She met his eyes and then said, 'I do hope that is so.'

She was obviously a decent woman who cared greatly for her brother, and he felt guilty for the bitter ugliness which his polite words cloaked. Clearly, she was unaware of the exact nature of past events.

'I will tell him you are here,' she at last nodded. 'I will see if he agrees to see you.'

Jared waited at the doorstep while she vanished

into the depths of the house. Within minutes she had returned.

'Yes, Mr. Harris,' she said, her voice showing a breathlessness. 'I have not seen him so elated for days. He said he will be delighted to see you.'

Jared managed a grateful smile, removed his hat and followed her into the cool interior of the hallway. Pictures of federal army officers, resplendent in dress uniform, adorned the walls. There was even a photograph of James Shafter himself, as a young lieutenant. He looked strikingly handsome, vastly different from the man Jared remembered.

He followed Ella up the wide staircase, momentarily recalling his own house in far-off Kentucky. In its way, it had been as grand as this residence, that is before it had been burned to the ground by crazed abolitionists. He swallowed hard, forcing the memory away and trying to display a casualness that was entirely contrary to his true feelings. On the landing, they passed beneath a beautiful glass chandelier. Jared felt conscious of his scruffy appearance, then told himself that the way he looked was of little consequence in view of his mission.

She opened a door at the far end of the landing, then stepped aside to allow him to enter. Jared took a deep breath, brushed his coat with his hand to feel the firmness of his gun beneath, then paced forward, knowing that this was the moment he had held in awe for so long. Coming into the bedroom, he was unable to stifle a shocked gasp.

The blinds were partially drawn, giving the room a ghostly ambience; the air within it seemed almost suffocating, smelling of sickness. Sitting next to the

bedstead was the ghoulish figure of James Morgan
Shafter. He was little more than a bag of bones; an
army tunic, displaying a major's gold leaves, was
draped about his shoulders and a blanket enveloped
his legs despite the heat of the day. He was wearing his
military campaign hat, pulled down to cover the cleft-
like scar that Jared knew lay across his forehead. He
was scarcely forty but his face was skeletal. When his
eyes seized on Jared, they were expressionless, like
those of a corpse.

'Damned Indians everywhere,' he said huskily, 'but
I'll fight 'em off, you'll see. Won't need your help,
Private Harris!'

'He's been very ill,' Ella Shafter said. 'You sit with
him for a while and talk over the old days. I'll fetch
some drinks.'

'Thank you,' Jared nodded. He had always known
that Shafter's injuries had twisted his mind, now he
sensed that this man was slipping down the slope to
outright insanity. He felt guilty that thoughts of
gunning him down had ever entered his head.

Ella Shafter had withdrawn, her footsteps sounding
as she went back down the stairs.

'Come here, Harris,' Shafter croaked. 'I've got something I want to give you.'

Jared hesitated, then he cursed himself. Why did he
hold this wreck of a man in such awe? The past was
over and done with, nothing could change that. Now all
that mattered was that some rapprochement was
reached, some conciliation that would enable each of
them to live out their remaining days at peace. Jared
stepped across the room.

'Kneel down,' Shafter snapped out, and then, as Jared hesitated, he added, 'That's an order, Private Harris.'

Jared dropped to one knee, feeling that he had to humour this sick man.

'Any Indians who came my way, I've shot down,' Shafter gasped, his eyes taking on a sudden shine. 'They say I'm a hero, you know.'

'Yes, I heard that,' Jared concurred.

Shafter grunted with satisfaction, moistening his lips with a quick dart of his tongue. 'Now I've only got one more duty to perform.'

'What's that?' Jared asked, uneasiness gripping him.

Shafter's lips widened into a scornful smile.

Jared heard Ella Shafter coming along the landing. Glasses were clinking on the tray she was holding. 'What duty do you have to perform?' he persisted.

'*Your execution!*' Shafter cried. He cast aside his blanket to reveal the revolver he was gripping. Before Jared could move, Shafter brought it up, clawed the trigger and fired point blank.

Miss Shafter had dropped her tray in alarm. As she rushed into the room, the echo of the detonation was bouncing off the walls. James Shafter was leaning back in his chair, a wisp of gunsmoke before him, and suddenly his laughter came.

Ella screamed, lifting her hands to her face in horror.

'Easier than killing Indians!' Shafter shouted.

Jared Harris was sprawled on his back, his blood darkening the carpet.

TWO

If Jared Harris could have related his experiences, he would have sworn that his misfortunes started the night in 1860 when the abolitionists torched his Kentucky plantation, and with it the fortune in baled cotton that was in the barns. Within minutes the entire place was aflame, he had been ruined and he and Annie were lucky to escape with their lives. All they could do was take flight and find refuge at the home of Jared's father, William Harris.

But there had been little respite for Jared, for the call to arms came.

The Southern-States were rebelling. No longer would they submit to domination from Washington, which to most was as far off as a foreign land. The final straw came with the election of Abraham Lincoln to the White House. He had spoken vociferously against slavery, no longer content to leave policy to individual states. The Southern states had always valued their autonomy, their own rule, while the Northern states were content to be united and governed from Washington. Now the North was striving to change the

15

very core of the Southern way of life, and the South would be bullied no more. Jared and the others were not fighting for the preservation of slavery, but for the freedom of choice.

Jared was six feet tall. Farm work had strengthened his muscles and given him a determination to succeed whatever the adversity. He was a reliable and thoughtful man with a ready sense of humour, and his face possessed strong features arranged in a pleasant fashion that in good times assumed a cheerful expression. He was liked by his fellows and in consequence, when the Eighth Kentucky was formed, he was elected Captain by the other volunteers, but he refused the rank, saying he would sooner serve as a private. In due course, a man he did not know, John Selby, became Captain, and Fred Carling, who worked on Selby's plantation, his sergeant.

April 1862 found the Eighth Kentucky Volunteers as part of the Confederate Army of the Mississippi under the command of General Albert Sidney Johnston. They had marched some twenty miles from their base at Corinth. The long lines of infantry, cavalry and trundling artillery had moved on roads that were little more than meandering cowpaths, and progress had been slowed by rainstorms, slippery mud, overloaded baggage-wagons and men's inexperience in marching. But now, in the small hours of Sunday morning, spirits were lifting. Spies had reported that the Federal encampment was scant miles ahead, at Pittsburgh Landing on the west bank of the Tennessee River, and indications were that the imminent attack was unsuspected.

Jared Harris had allowed himself a glimpse at the smiling face of his wife Annie. Her eyes never lost their sparkle, even as they gazed at him from the tintype photograph that he carefully shielded from the moisture dripping from the overhead branches. Her faintly freckled face fairly glowed in the flickering light of the campfire. At night he slept in a blanket that she had meticulously embroidered. His love for Annie charged him with energy and urged him to show the utmost resolution. This was his contribution to bringing the war to a successful conclusion, thus drawing closer the day he could restore his plantation in Kentucky.

Hearing the approach of Captain Selby, he wrapped the photograph in its protective tissue and returned it to his pocket.

Selby was a tall man with angular features and his thin face was constantly flushed with hatred for the Federals. It was his very fervour to engage in war that had gained him his rank. Rumour had it that his father had been butchered by Yankee marauders, his wife and twin daughters raped and murdered, but he never spoke of it. Now, he had attended a conference of officers.

'We're to mount an attack at six-thirty, catch the enemy before reinforcements arrive,' he imparted to his men. 'Remember, you are here, not to injure the Yanks or take them prisoner, but to *kill* them – as many as you can. Kindly make sure you are ready.'

'Yes, suh!' Sergeant Carling responded.

Harris did not like Selby but he respected him, and he felt this was reciprocated.

The men of the Eighth Kentucky had been raised in

haste. While Captain Selby and Sergeant Carling had uniforms, the men, mostly farm boys, had not. They carried a variety of smooth-bore muskets and in appearance resembled a mob of armed citizens. Harris glanced around at their faces. Some of them he had known for years. Others had scarcely reached puberty. Most of them had never travelled more than a hundred miles from their homes, never seen a big city. He wondered how many would be dead within the next twenty-four hours. Now, they made sorry attempts to show bravado, to jest, but he knew that inwardly they had similar thoughts to his own. At Corinth, they had been instilled with a sense of patriotism and a determination not to let each other down.

At the appointed time, the Eighth Kentucky took up position in the battalion that was to form the first line of attack. Captain Selby marched stiff-backed ahead of his men, his sabre drawn, an urgent desire to engage the enemy reflected in the briskness of his movements. The moon, partially hidden by cloud, brought little light to the forest and many of the paths under the trees were in total darkness. Cold rain filtered down through the branches, yet now, even in the night, men sweated beneath their coats at the prospect of the coming fight, and cursed at the hordes of night insects that pestered them.

In all, there were nine brigades deployed. They advanced stealthily, yet with the progress of so many men, some racket was inevitable: startled birds rose noisily from their roosts, twigs snapped underfoot, and orders, albeit issued in restrained Southern voices, seemed inordinately loud. Several times brass-bound musket-butts clattered against tree trunks, bringing a swarm of sibilant curses that seemed louder than the offending noises. They had been warned that the success of the attack hinged on the element of surprise being maintained.

Jared Harris felt slick with sweat. The tangled thickets and underbrush caused the formation to become extended and broken, and he was constantly struggling to keep close to the shadowy figures of his fellow Kentuckians, at the same time wondering how near they were getting to the tented encampment of the enemy. He felt a crushing anxiety to get on with the fight.

As the first glimmer of dawn streaked the sky, word was passed down to form a skirmish line, and as this was achieved they broke free of the trees. Ahead stretched a muddy field, some two hundred yards across, its surface pockmarked with the lighter hue of many puddles. Jared gazed to its far side, saw how the high grasses swayed in the dawn breeze, then the paleness of the grass became darker as if ants were spreading through it.

At that moment, somebody cried, 'There they are!' and a collective gasp escaped men's throats. The ants changed to a thickening line of Federals, the early light catching the metal of their guns as they advanced on to the field.

An order was passed down the Confederate line, repeated, and men went to ground, kneeling in the oozing mud, fumbling to bring their weapons into their shoulders and open fire, sparks of orange illuminating the gloomy dawn.

*

At the Union Camp during the preceding night hours, Major James Shafter had bristled as he recalled the statement issued by his commander, General Sherman, when scouts had reported an enemy presence. *You all get scared too easily. There is no enemy nearer than Corinth.* Shafter knew that Sherman had been accused of overreacting on previous occasions. Now the general appeared determined not to face such criticisms again. Indeed, not even routine patrols had been sent out to watch the roads from Corinth, nor had defensive entrenchments been dug. Instead, men lounged casually in their tented camp near the simple log meetinghouse which was Shiloh Church.

James Shafter was a regular officer, a good-looking, likeable and efficient man whose courage had been proved at Bull Run. Just after midnight, he walked through rain to the tent of his commander, Colonel Jessup. After Shafter expressed his concerns, Jessup agreed that what the scouts were this time reporting could well be true.

'We'll have to do a reconnaissance on our own initiative,' he said. 'I'll probably get my ass kicked for this, but I'm sure the Johnny Rebs are closer than Sherman reckons.' He pondered for a moment, then added, 'Take three companies, see what you can find.'

Shafter nodded, saluted and departed.

As dawn agitated the sky, it was his three companies that encountered the vanguard of the Rebel attack at Frealey Field. Both sides exchanged fire, but the range was too great for heavy casualties to be inflicted, although one Union officer was slightly wounded by a stray bullet. Shafter now perceived that his duty was to fall back and warn General Sherman that the enemy had shown up in force. He therefore ordered his command to retreat.

Seeing the enemy withdrawing, the Confederate force rose to its feet and advanced across the muddy stretch of field. Those who had bayonets had fixed them to their muskets. The surprise of their attack had now been lost, but having seen the Yankees falling back, they moved rapidly through the increasing rain, undaunted by the slippery ground. Their pace continued, passing through wooded land, until they saw the white of tents ahead and it appeared that the enemy were intending to make some sort of stand. Screaming their Rebel Cry like fiends, they charged in, the Eighth Kentucky in the forefront. At first the Union resistance seemed erratic as men rushed from their tents, pulling on their tunics, grabbing their guns. They immediately fell back to the area adjacent to the log cabin church.

The scent of victory spurred the Confederates on, and soon they were engaged in close hand-to-hand conflict. Jared Harris was in the thick of it. There was no time to reload muskets after the initial volley and he found himself swinging his weapon by the barrel, clouting men aside, aware of skulls being cracked. Other men were battling with their fists or chopping and stabbing at each other with bayonets, screaming, struggling, dying. It was a vicious exchange with no quarter given, tents being trampled to the ground in the turmoil. All trace of order was lost. It was left to each individual to further his cause. Jared stumbled

over the fallen of both sides and there was no time to
differentiate. The crash of muskets thundered about
his ears, the whistle of bullets was constant. Through
the gunsmoke, he glimpsed Sergeant Carling doubled
over on the ground, his belly slit, trying, with bloody
hands, to stem the blueness of his guts from spilling
out.

Jared felt the swish of something heavy and twisted
to the side as a musket-butt brushed his head.

He could hear Captain Selby screaming, 'Advance!
Advance!'

But Jared could not go forward because he was
locked in combat with a Yankee corporal, saw for an
instant the man's bloodshot eyes, bereft of reason, lost
in the berserk savagery of the battle. The Kentuckian
swung his musket, gripping the barrel with blood slippery hands, to catch him across the side of the skull
and send him spinning away. He glanced around for
Selby, but he was nowhere to be seen amid the mêlée
and smoke.

He tripped over some tent-ropes; he scrambled up,
somehow finding time to recharge his musket. He shot
into a group of blue uniforms, saw the group break –
and then he became aware of a slackening in the
conflict and realized that the enemy were yet again
falling back, driven out of their own encampment; but
the cost had been high. As the exchange of gunfire
decreased, the groaning, the screams, the cursing of
the wounded became awesome.

Jared searched about, trying to locate his fellow
Kentuckians, and gradually they drew together, their
faces grimed with blood and sweat, their eyes wild.

Many were missing, but there was no time for roll-call. Captain Selby appeared, his hat gone, his hair awry. As he waved his sabre, urging them forward, Jared saw that its blade was shiny with blood.

'We've got 'em on the run!' Selby yelled. 'Let's finish 'em off!'

THREE

Major James Morgan Shafter had been sickened by the turn of events. He cursed Sherman's stupidity in not taking proper precautions against attack. It had seemed obvious that the Confederates would not remain at Corinth. But now it was too late and defeat was staring them in the eye. Shafter had seen his command decimated. He himself had fought bravely, though he sensed it was a lost cause. He was urging what remained of his men across an open stretch of ground towards the cover of a peach-orchard, pausing to hasten a straggler. Glancing over his shoulder, he saw the devilish figures of Rebels surging in pursuit, so close that he glimpsed the murderous lust in their eyes, even the yellow and grey of their flag and upon it 8TH KENTUCKY VOLUNTEERS. He waved his sabre in defiance.

And at that moment a minié ball caught him high on the forehead, sent him stumbling down with blood blinding him. He lay in the mud, feeling that his brains were seeping out through a hole in his skull. He could feel the ground shuddering beneath him, pounded by

many feet. He fought against the red mists of unconsciousness, sensing that he was dying – and suddenly,
intruding into his agony, he heard voices around him,
Southern voices, crazy, angry voices – and somebody
yelled, 'Finish 'im off, Captain!'

'With pleasure . . . with pleasure.' And Shafter felt a
menacing presence looming over him, cold, hard . . .
and the boots slammed into his helpless body, into his
spine, tossing him about like a rag toy . . . on and on
and on, the crazed scream matching each kick: *'That's
for my wife, that's for my father, that's for my little
girls,'* and then the redness of Shafter's semi-
consciousness gave way to impenetrable black.

Twenty minutes later, as Captain Selby set about
reforming the survivors of the Eighth Kentucky to
continue the assault, a sniper's bullet caught him, the
ball slamming into his chest. Jared caught him as he
fell, staggering under the surprising weight but lower-
ing him gently down, finding cover in the fold of the
ground in case the sniper fired again. There was little
else he could do for his captain. He died in his arms,
coughing up frothy blood. He had not liked this man
very much, for he had been bitter and merciless, caring
for little apart from his personal crusade of vengeance,
but seeing his life ebb away brought tears to Jared's
eyes.

Scarcely had he risen from the body, when somebody
shouted that General Johnston himself had been killed
and that General Beauregard, his second-in-command,
had assumed command of the Confederate force.

Jared became aware that the surviving, battle-scarred men of the Eighth Kentucky were grouping around him. With both captain and sergeant killed, he was the natural leader amongst them. There was no time for contemplation, and he accepted the responsibility. Selby had wanted them to continue the advance, and that was the way it must be. He relieved the dead officer of his bloodstained sabre, pistol and ammunition, searched his pockets for any personal documents for return to his family, but found nothing. He then called his men together, and within a few minutes they were going forward again.

The Yankee forces were making another stand. This time along a sunken road that cleaved the forest. Again, the crackle of intense fire bludgeoned the air and this continued throughout the next hours. Jared and his line were sheltering in the trees, directing musket fire on to the road. Shots whizzed all around them, clipping bark from the trees and eliciting grunts of pain as men were hit. The air was acrid with gunsmoke. Presently the exchange of fire became desultory and a stalemate developed. But it was only the lull before the storm. In the late afternoon, a new element was introduced as the boom of Confederate artillery sounded, coming from the rear, filling the sky with screaming missiles and men's nostrils with the taint of cordite. Fire was being brought to bear on the road.

The commotion of bursting shells along the sunken road was causing havoc amongst the defenders, and again it was obvious that the Union forces were giving way. The ground was slippery with rain and blood and littered with discarded muskets, caps, belts, cartridge boxes, torn knapsacks, battered canteens. Everything was perforated with shot. Men had been stricken down in solid ranks, the faces of the wounded twisted with the jagged thrusts of the unbearable. Their cursing, blaspheming cries for water were relentless. Medical orderlies scrambled amongst the injured and dead in the hopeless task of trying to bring comfort, caring for men of both sides. The carnage was sickening. But now the light was going, the artillery barrage had diminished and the steady hiss of rain dripping through the leafy fronds grew louder.

Jared anticipated that a further order to advance would come, but instead the word was passed down the line that they were to withdraw. He felt disheartened just when, it seemed, that final victory was in their grasp. But he rose and directed the men to join the rest of the force as a general fall-back was commenced. Men helped their wounded comrades; even so, many were left in the trees for later recovery by the overworked stretcher parties. The surgeons would be busy that night. Where there was hope of survival, they would saw limbs and probe for bullets. There would be no time to tend the dying.

The cost to the Eighth Kentucky had been crippling. As well as losing their captain and sergeant, a good third of the men failed to answer the roll-call. Many of these had been close friends of Jared. As they went into camp that night, the volunteers formally elected Jared as their new captain, and this time he accepted the appointment, believing that if he refused he would have let the others down. A new sergeant was also elected. But there was no mood for celebration; the hideousness of the day lay too heavily upon them. And to increase the melancholy, spies reported in with news that the Union forces had been reinforced and were preparing to advance the next morning. In view of this, General Beauregard ordered his army to retreat to the original base at Corinth. Beauregard himself moved through the lines, attempting to lift the spirits of his battle-weary command. The Yankees, he said, had been given a bloody nose and would know now that the war was not going to be a short-term affair. Jared Harris appreciated that the general took time to seek him out and congratulate him on his promotion.

Major James Shafter had no recollection beyond the moment when he had been kicked as he lay helpless, each kick seeming like smothering earth being shovelled upon him as he lay in an open grave. Now he regained consciousness, at first feeling no pain, just an incredible lightness of the head. Flies buzzed about him; in fact everywhere seemed thick with flies. He was afraid of breathing them into his nostrils. Big, black flies, no doubt depositing their maggoty offspring indiscriminately. A sickening stench pervaded, a combination of vomit, excrement and the effluvia of bloody wounds, all backed by the smothering sweetness of chloroform.

His fumbling senses tuned into the sounds around him – the groans, the endless profanity of the wounded. Near him a man was grinding his teeth relentlessly. From further away, he caught the clink of surgical instruments, and voices conversing in weary tones.

They were discussing the merits of whether a man's leg should be amputated above or below the knee. Shortly agreement was reached and he heard the rasp of a saw. Shafter realized that one of his senses was missing. He could not see. Even so, instinct told him he was in a large tent, and that it was a field hospital.

Then the pain swept up on him – a headache of slamming intensity. He tried to move but grunted as agony flamed down his spine. Simultaneously he became aware of other pains probing into every nook of his body. He wondered if he had undergone leg amputation, but he had not the strength to examine himself. He was satisfied that at least his hands were still attached to his wrists. He had never been one for cursing, but now he mouthed every foul word he could think of. He cursed the war, the cruel fate that had befallen him – and worst of all he cursed those who had reduced him to this pitiful state.

But now the pain, grasping his skull in a grip of iron, became intolerable. He cried out, his voice a hoarse rasp that could not compete with the cries of many others. Eventually he subsided, defeated. Nobody came to help him, to tell him what was happening. All he could do was withdraw into his own world and surrender to his suffering. Maybe, his fevered mind thought, maybe I am already dead. If he was already dead and this place was hell, then it was aptly named. For a time he battled against the forceful claims of unconsciousness, feeling a desperate urge to fight off the surgeons if they lifted him on to their butchery table. But eventually his senses ebbed away and he descended into merciful insensibility.

*

Captain Jared Harris's personal war was to last only a
further twelve months. After the Battle of Shiloh, the
Eighth Kentucky was reformed and marched along the
Savannah roads to the main Confederate camp at
Pickens. Here, their generals attempted to rally the
morale of the army and prepare them for another
battle that lay ahead.

It would be at a place called Gettysburg.

Thus, on June 30 of the following year, the
Confederate and Union armies, drawn like moths to a
flame, faced each other across the lush farmlands at
Gettysburg. For two days they blasted each other with
artillery. On the third day of the battle, the Eighth
Kentucky took part in the ill-fated charge upon the
high ground known as Cemetery Ridge, where the
Yankees were entrenched. The Union artillery opened
up, firing canister, ripping away huge gaps in the
Confederate advance, but these gaps closed up and the
charge continued. At last the decimated attackers
climbed the Union barricade and became engaged in
grappling hand-to-hand combat. Men fought like
devils, ploughing into each other, teeth bared, eyes
glinting hatred.

Jared Harris, striking out with his sabre, feeling it
meet the resistance of flesh, found himself surrounded
by men in blue uniforms. The noise was bedlam. He
considered it a miracle that he had survived this far,
but now he sensed that his time had come and the only
regret in him was for Annie, waiting longingly for his
return. He determined to die with honour. Lead was

whining about his head; blows were bouncing off him. One man lunged at him with his bayonet, but Jared warded it off with such force that he snapped his sabre. Then he felt a numbing impact in his back, was propelled forward and knew that a bullet had struck him, cutting his breath.

Beyond that . . . nothing.

FOUR

Jared Harris found himself slumped in a sort of wooden corral in which cattle would normally be kept. The rain was falling steadily. He realized he was lying in a puddle. He made an effort to move, but in so doing awoke a sharp pain in his chest. Other men, in blood-stained grey, maybe twenty or more, were sprawled around him. One of them, a corporal with his front teeth broken, turned and said, 'From all accounts you was mighty lucky, Cap'n. Bullet passed clean through you.'

Jared managed a nod, then attempted a breath and pain came again.. He could only breathe in shallow gasps. 'Where are we?' he managed to get out.

His companion paused to spit, then said, 'Prisoners. At least we're away from the bullets, but I don't reckon our long-term prospects is too damned rosy.'

Jared cursed. He felt bruised and battered and wondered if his lung had taken the bullet. He could see that blood had soaked the front of his shirt which bore out the corporal's opinion that the bullet had passed clean through. Even so, he felt as if he had a tight steel

32

band around his ribs, pressing inward against his lungs, what was left of them. He groaned, wondering why the Good Lord had chosen him to survive, when so many other men had gone to their graves.

At that moment a Union officer and a half-dozen bluecoats entered the stockade and ordered them to stand up. Jared attempted to comply, would have fallen back had his companion not supported him.

The Union officer started to speak: 'You Rebels are prisoners of war and will be treated accordingly, as long as you behave yourselves. If you attempt to escape I have given my men orders to shoot you down without hesitation, so be warned. We don't love you one little bit and won't feel any grief. In fact it will make our burden easier. Now form up and prepare for a long march!'

A ripple of cursing went through the battle-weary Rebels. Six officers, Jared included, were bundled to the front as the column was formed two abreast. He was in acute pain but he determined not to complain. He did not fancy any knife-mad surgeons, let alone those of the Union. Soon they were being marched from the compound, enough Yankees hovering around them, their guns ready, to make any attempt at escape inadvisable. But Jared promised himself that when the opportunity arose, he would take to his heels. It had never been his intention to finish the war this way. Death maybe, but as a prisoner, no.

As they plodded along rough forest tracks, sloshing through puddles and mud, he felt light-headed. He cursed himself for being captured, and wounded into the bargain. His breathing was difficult, the pain from the bullet hole sickening, but to take his mind from it he thought about Annie back at the farm in Kentucky. They had been married for just six months, the first bloom of their love was still fresh and vibrant. She was the daughter of the town banker, and had taken to being a plantation wife as readily as a duck to water. Jared Harris had come into a thousand acres of prime land, dedicated to producing cotton, when ill health had forced his father to retire three years back. Now the war had changed everything, but the prospect of one day returning home was the bright star which Jared was determined to follow. He was still alive. What else mattered?

But determination was not sufficient to keep his legs going. Maybe a lesser man than Jared would have collapsed many miles earlier. As it was, he kept going for twelve miles until sheer weakness and exhaustion, coupled with his enforced shallow breathing, claimed him and he fell before his jaded companions could support him. The detail made camp shortly afterwards and he was dumped down with his back against an oak tree. For a time he listened to the hum of voices around him. Most of his fellow prisoners were silent, but the voices of the Yankee guards showed a jubilance. Apparently Gettyshurg had been an overwhelming victory for the Union. The casualties had been massive on both sides, but the Confederacy had fared much worse and General Robert E. Lee had been forced to withdraw.

'Open your tunic up, Captain, let's have a look at that wound.'

Jared raised his eyes and saw an officer gazing

down at him. He was carrying a leather bag and was obviously a doctor. An orderly stood beside him. Jared was tempted to refuse treatment, but had not the breath to do so and he submitted to the order.

The doctor hurried him along, having little time to meet all that was demanded of him. He pulled open Jared's shirt, peeled back the tatters of his undershirt from the bloody hole of the wound, back and front, then he produced his stethoscope from the leather bag and listened to his patient's chest.

He looked at Jared, his expression grim, nonetheless his words were welcome.

'Seems you're a lucky man,' he said. 'That bullet must've missed your lungs by a fraction and passed between your ribs. You'll survive as long as the wound doesn't go bad. Plenty of rest is what you need. I think at least you'll get the opportunity to sit out the rest of this goddamned war.' He turned to his orderly. 'Get a dressing around him.'

'Yessir!'

The orderly lacked the doctor's gentle touch. He roughly wound bandage round Jared's chest, cursing him to hold still.

'Where are we heading for?' Jared winced.

'Prison camp at Winnema. But I guess you, being a goddamn officer, will get special treatment.'

'I don't want special treatment,' Jared gasped.

The orderly fastened the bandage with a knot. 'You won't get no say in the matter.'

Next day they started out again, trudging through the Virginia countryside. The sun was hot and the birds sang brightly in the trees, and the guards reck-

oned they were on a good thing, having left behind the
blood and gore of the battlefield. Maybe some of the
prisoners felt the same way, though the prospect of a
Yankee prison camp was a dismal thought. But for
Jared Harris the march was a nightmare as he struggled against the pain from his wound.

'Maybe the war will be over soon,' the man next to
him commented. 'Lee's not going to take the defeat at
Gettysburg sitting down. Lee'll come back, take
Washington, then we'll all be free to go home.'

Jared nodded, but his heart was full of doubts.

The prison camp at Winnema was encircled by a fifteen-
foot high stockade. The place was bleak and cruel, bursting at the seams with disgruntled Rebels and infested
with rats. The prisoners lived in crowded tents,
surrounded by open latrines, and the conditions in
which the officers were kept, though segregated, were
no different from those of the non-commissioned ranks.
When the sun shone, the interiors of the tents became
oven-like. When it rained, the water dripped through,
turning everything into a quagmire. Death rates were
high, mainly from gangrene, pneumonia and poor nour-
ishment, and bloodhounds were kennelled nearby to
track down any runaways; they barked relentlessly,
night and day.

Jared was consigned to the dingy hut which was the
prison hospital and there, surrounded by other
patients of mixed fortune, he received some attention
from a harassed doctor. After three days he was
thrown out to take his chances with his fellow officers.
Over a period of a month, a month of crushing bore-

dom and frustration, he made a steady recovery from his wound, somehow avoiding the infection that was all around.

FIVE

She was twenty-one, a slim and pretty girl with red hair. She wore a pert pill-box hat and veil. She found the gaunt old building in Jefferson Street. This was the central hospital for wounded officers of the Union. She was engaged to Major James Shafter. Theirs had been a whirlwind and passionate courtship. She believed him to be the most handsome and chivalrous man alive and he had swept her off her feet. But the war had interrupted their plans.

'It will be over in a few weeks,' he had told her. 'The Southern states will collapse like a pack of cards,' and she had believed him and longed for the day when she could become his wife.

Now she realized he had been wrong. She nervously entered the hospital and her eyes were drawn to scenes more awful than any she had imagined possible. Her father had warned her against coming, that she was of too delicate a temperament. The place smelt of death and flies buzzed everywhere. She saw men sprawled on beds, their stumped legs and arms swathed in grimy bandages. Their groans filled her ears.

She wished she had heeded her father's advice; she should not have come. Even so, she found the courage to ask for Major Shafter. On the third attempt, she was directed along a dark corridor to a large end-room. Just inside the door a man was lying upon a bed. Both his legs had been amputated. Somehow, she could not tear her eyes away from him. He was so still; his skin had a waxen, yellow taint about it. She felt certain he was dead. She also felt certain it was not James.

A man using a crutch appeared at her side.

'Who do you want, my dear?'

'Major Shafter,' she whispered huskily. 'Major James Shafter.'

He nodded. 'By the far window.' He gestured with his crutch towards the corner of the room.

And here she found him. She would never have recognized him. His face and head were heavily bandaged. He was either asleep or unconscious, she could not be sure which. At least he was breathing, for she could see the rise and fall of his chest. The man she had spoken to previously stood beside her.

'Is he dying?' she inquired.

He shook his head. 'No, but he'll never be the same again. He'll most likely lose his sight. Are you his wife?'

'Oh no,' she said, and then she added another, 'No.'

The man nodded understandingly and then hopped away, leaning heavily on his crutch.

She stayed at James Shafter's bedside for ten minutes. She recalled the fine photograph they had had taken. He had looked so resplendent in his uniform. She had felt so proud of him. Now. . . .

She emitted a pitiful sigh. She wiped her eyes with a lace handkerchief. Yes, her father had been right. It had not been sensible to come here. She was desperately out of place. She turned away, walked down the long corridor with her eyes averted, and left the hospital.

Later, her father advised her that she should break off the relationship. Sadly, he said, James Shafter would now be no good for any woman and he would not be able to give her the future she deserved. She must look elsewhere for a husband. Her father was right. She carefully composed a letter, making her words as gentle as possible and hoped that the person who read it to James would show compassion. She enclosed her engagement ring, neatly wrapped in tissue paper. She wept that night, but over the subsequent weeks her sorrow grew less intense.

The bloody encounter at Gettysburg proved to be the benchmark of the war. The Confederacy's brave attempt to march on Richmond had been repulsed, with huge losses. The flower of Robert E. Lee's manpower had fallen, his army decimated. The Union had greater numbers, greater reserves, and now at last the tide of the war began to turn. Other battles came and went, but the Southern army was falling back.

At the Winnema prison camp in Maryland news filtered through to the prisoners. At first Jared Harris refused to believe it, but gradually he accepted, with a heavy heart, the truth of what he heard. As more Confederate prisoners crowded in, the grim news was confirmed.

He had been lucky in that he had survived the bullet that had passed through his chest. His breathing had slowly improved. He exercised his lungs and rib-cage every day, though a constricting sensation in his chest returned in moments of stress. He longed to encounter some familiar faces from his own area, and thus gain news of his wife Annie. But his enquiries met with blank faces and shaken heads. He wondered if she was ill and how she was coping, and frustration grew in him.

In the officers' section of the camp, the conditions worsened due to overcrowding. He and four of his fellow prisoners hatched up a plan for escape, had started to dig a tunnel under the enclosure. Just when hope of getting away was flaring in them a guard discovered their work and their plans came tumbling down. As punishment, they were stripped of officer status and consigned to the non-commissioned enclosure. Thereafter he suffered the same miserable existence as the lowest rank, working long, back-aching hours in labour gangs, chipping away in the nearby granite pits with pick-axe and shovel, constantly under the surveillance of armed guards. They had already shot two men attempting to escape. Jared realized he would have to bide his time. But events took a surprising turn.

One day the message was passed down that the Union government had decided to recruit from the prison camps. Men were needed to join the Union Army as so-called 'Galvanized Yankees'. They would not be used to fight their own kind, but sent to the far-off Indian frontier to make the trails safe from red depredation. At first the thought of donning a blue uniform was abhorrent to Jared, but then the opportunity of getting away from the stinking hole of this prison was too much to resist. In consequence he signed a pledge that he would serve the Union faithfully, after which he was warned that should he attempt to escape, the penalty would be the firing squad, with no mercy given. He knew he must take his chances.

The bandages were removed from the head of James Shafter three weeks after the visit of the girl he would have married. He was unaware that she had come to the hospital, but he had grieved when her letter was read to him. As the dressings were removed from his eyes, the light seemed to lance into him, causing sharp pain. The doctors were surprised and delighted by the fact that his vision had not been lost. Everything was blurred, but a doctor told him that within a few days his sight should return to normal. But his severe headache persisted, his skull felt like a coconut that had been cracked open and roughly tied together with string. He was afraid to reach up with his fingers and explore its surface. His cracked ribs still caused him great discomfort. And shafts of pain shot up his back each time he moved.

'Vertebrae chipped to bits,' the doctor explained. 'That Johnny Reb must've been twisted with hatred to kick hell out of you like that.'

Considering everything, the medical man was pleased with his progress and called him one of the lucky ones. He told him that within six months there was no reason why he could not return to military service.

His sister Ella came to visit him and stayed for a good hour. She was five years younger than him, an efficient, compassionate woman who would have made a good wife for any man, yet she had never married, having remained at home to care for their widowed father until his death just prior to the war. Today she chatted brightly, telling him how the flowers were blooming in the Idaho meadows. Presently, she spoke of the war, saying how the tide of battle was turning in the Union's favour. He had little strength to respond, but he tried to smile. Even so, he sensed that her cheerful manner was a façade, that she was trying desperately to cheer him up, and once, when she turned away, he saw her make a quick dab at a tear in her eye.

Eventually, as she was preparing to leave, he asked her if she had a mirror in her bag. She shook her head firmly, then she leaned forward, kissed him on the cheek and departed.

The following day he asked the doctor if he might borrow a mirror. The medical man hesitated, then he nodded and an hour later a nurse brought him one. She turned away before he raised it to examine his face. She was half-way across the ward when she heard his cry of anguish.

She shuddered. But she had seen worse cases. At least he had survived.

SIX

There were four 'Galvanized Yankees' assigned to Colonel Carrington's 14th Regiment of Infantry. Jared Harris was one. They had been issued with dark-blue shell jackets, light-blue wool trousers and forage caps with floppy crowns. They were also issued with black shoes which did not differentiate between the right and left foot, and Jared was obliged to soak his in hot water in order to make them fit. He gritted his teeth as he put on his blue uniform for the first time. For so long the word 'bluebelly' had been tantamount to a curse. Now he was one of them. But, he told himself, as long as he was not required to fight against the Confederacy, he would honour his oath of allegiance.

He knew he would get no opportunity to return home. He had not heard from Annie for months, but now he penned a letter, expressing his love and devotion and telling her not to worry about him and that the day would eventually dawn when they could resume normal life. He did not know if the letter would ever be delivered to Kentucky but he prayed so. His mind flooded with thoughts of the green meadows of home, the winding streams, of walking hand in hand with Annie. He recalled the happiness of her laughter and the way her eyes sparkled with fun. And then there had been the unstinting warmth of her body and kisses – and the thought made him groan, so that it seemed hard physical labour to turn his mind to other things, but he knew he must or he would die of frustration.

So far as he could make out, Carrington's regiment had been ordered to march into the wilderness and construct several forts along the new Bozeman Trail. This led to distant Virginia City and the Montana goldfields in the north and a flood of prospectors and settlers were desperate to use the new trail, instead of the much longer Idaho route. But the Sioux Indians were objecting strongly to white encroachment through territory which they claimed as theirs. Carrington's orders were to make the trail safe.

One day a dispatch came through with the news that the Confederacy had surrendered at the Appomattox Courthouse. Lee had finally thrown in his hand, his army too crippled to prolong the war. Jared wept that night, wept for all his friends and other good men who had died to defend their cause, but among his blue-coated fellows there was great celebration and a limited measure of liquor was allowed them.

On 14 April 1865, the regiment marched out from Fort Kearney in Nebraska with the band playing. Jared was aware of the resentment from his new comrades. His Southern accent made him stand out like a sore thumb, and the fact that he had been an officer increased the resentment. But his skin was thick and he told himself that he was just serving his time until he could go home.

For days they marched into the sparsely populated Wyoming wilderness, far, far away from the battle-fields in the East. The country seemed one of endless horizons consisting of pine-forested hills, wide stretches of prairie and fast-flowing rivers.

Jared penned another letter to Annie, telling her what had happened to him and that he was in good health and would be home just as soon as he could. Meanwhile, she was not to worry, for there appeared to be little danger out here in the wilderness. Writing gave him the feeling of being in communication with her, though there was no guarantee she would ever read his words. He knew she would be relieved to hear that he was no longer risking his life in the Civil War.

Carrington's command was made up of some 500 officers and enlisted men, mostly foot-soldiers, complete with a band of some twenty musicians, surveyors, carpenters, a herd of cattle, a number of wives and camp-followers. Eight weeks after starting out, they reached Fort Laramie, arriving at the same time that a conference with wild Indians was in progress. Apparently several important chiefs were in attendance, including Red Cloud. Negotiators had come from Washington to represent the government.

Jared glimpsed the dark faces of the Indians, painted with lines of bright ochre. Most of them carried rifles. They wore headdresses of gaudy feathers and looked truly wild, a stark contrast to the military men and the negotiators in their black coats and top hats.

The Indians had pitched their tents to the south of the fort, a vast spread of white-skinned conical abodes supported on crossed poles. From the outlets, a haze of smoke lifted into the blue sky. The pony herd grazed on the ground closer to the outlying buildings of the fort.

The powwow continued for three days, but was eventually terminated. Jared heard how Red Cloud and his followers had stormed out, vowing that they would never submit to white encroachment. It was incredible how quickly the Indian village was dismantled and vanished into the wilderness. Red Cloud had threatened that any whites who proceeded past Crazy Woman's Fork of the Powder River would be killed.

Before leaving Fort Laramie, Jared left his letter with the post corporal.

The regiment continued its march, passing through meadows of wild flax that matched the sky, and over which pronghorn deer bounded away. Fast babbling streams sparkled in the sunshine, meadow larks shrilled and jack rabbits paused to watch the column, cocking their black-tipped ears.

Jared was no stranger to enforced marches, his feet having long been hardened. Like those around him, he felt little fear from the Indian threats. The Army was confident that it was strong enough to deal with a few ill-disciplined natives. But Red Cloud had been underestimated. Ahead, awaited a bloodbath.

All around the mountains loomed, snow-tipped and glinting in the spring sunshine. To Jared it seemed that they were progressing into virgin land, previously unsullied by the white man. Colonel Carrington, mounted at the front of the column, frequently consulted maps and conferred with his officers and scouts. They saw no sign of Indians, though Jared suspected that the column was under surveillance. There were too many hiding places in this country. The women rode in white-topped wagons, and every effort was made to prevent stragglers. Scouts roamed out, bringing in game for the cooking-pots. The regiment forded the Powder River at Crazy Woman's Fork, hardly giving a thought to the fact that this was the point beyond which Red Cloud had promised death to white trespassers.

Guards were mounted regularly and Jared found himself doing more than his fair share. He was still taunted by the others, but he took it in his stride and never retaliated. The sergeant in charge of his section, a man known as 'Horse' Millard, was a square-built, loud-mouthed man from the New York Bowery. His face seemed constantly flushed. He had a reputation as a heavy drinker. He was a harsh disciplinarian, foul-mouthed and unfair. He seemed to delight in picking on Jared, using every opportunity to impose extra duty and unpleasant tasks.

On 13 June, the column was halted between the forks of the Little Piney and Big Piney Creeks. This was an area of luxuriant grassland, a sort of natural saucer surrounded by hills. Towering above them, in the west, were the Bighorn Mountains. Colonel Carrington had found a spot which he considered suitable to build his fort. Jared glimpsed the colonel pacing out distances on the ground, discussing with his officers where buildings would be erected.

That night the regiment pitched its tents and rested up in readiness for the hard work that was to start next day, but there was little rest for Jared. Sergeant Millard placed him on night-time guard and early-morning fatigues, digging latrines, for what he called dumb insolence. Jared merely nodded and watched the sergeant swagger off to the wagon that he and his wife occupied. Millard was one of the few enlisted men to be accompanied by his wife. She worked as a laundress. Jared had taken little notice of her apart from the fact that she appeared a mere slip of a girl, considerably younger than her horse of a husband. She seemed to live in fear of him. By the bruising that showed on the side of her face, she had ample cause. But nobody else seemed at all concerned by what Millard did to his wife.

Next day, detachments went out to cut timber from the forests, hauling it back on wagons, and the sound of hammers and saws filled the air. Jared worked unloading the quartermaster's supplies, stacking them within the perimeter of the area on the south side of main fort. Men toiled and sweated, stripped to the waist, while the wives of officers stood in their pretty dresses shaded by their parasols. Other women took basketfuls of soiled clothing down to the stream for washing.

Jared noticed that Millard's wife was among them, and, just for a second, her eye caught his and she smiled, and for the first time he noticed how white her skin seemed beneath the mop of unruly, curling hair. She was thin and her narrow face had a sharpness of feature. Her mouth was full-lipped and faintly curved, showing her front teeth which were set well apart. But it was her wide and roaming eyes that dominated her, and somehow gave her a frail prettiness. She moved with the furtiveness of a frightened bird. But such considerations were no business of his, and he turned away and carried on with his work before he was accused of slacking.

Word was passed round that the new military post would be known as Fort Phil Kearny, named after a general. Over the next weeks, the palisade began to take shape and buildings rose, the regimental head-quarters being first, followed by the quartermaster's establishment. Next came the officers' accommodation, the men's barrack blocks and the post hospital. On a lofty pole, the Union Flag provided a flash of colour against the green hillsides. Jared felt a pang of shame that he now served the flag of an enemy he had fought so hard to defeat.

Now scouts were reporting back that the presence of Indians had been discovered in the vicinity and shortly after this Sioux were spotted on the ridges adjacent to the fort, silhouetted against the sky, waving their rifles in defiance.

At the fort was a photographer who was constantly setting up his camera on a tripod and taking pictures of the men, the wives, and the fort in general. 'Keeping a record for posterity,' he proclaimed. He had no fear of the Indians and took to leaving the fort and walking the surrounding hills, taking pictures as he went. One evening he did not return and next day a detail discovered his body. The sight was horrific. He had been stripped naked. His corpse resembled a pin cushion with arrows, and his genitals had been excised and stuffed into his mouth.

Now the sense of danger that surrounded the fort heightened. Timber-cutting parties went out daily into the surrounding pineries and soon attacks on these became a regular occurrence, the Indians surging out of the forest, shooting down any men in exposed positions and then vanishing before retaliation could be effected. Casualties became frequent and the post hospital was busy. Jared took his turn, sometimes felling the pines and sometimes standing guard while others worked, his life made extra tiresome by the persistent overbearing manner of Sergeant Millard. For some reason this man hated his guts and this was to be made even worse by future events.

The fort was now almost completed. It consisted of two major stockades which were linked together, and there was a watch-tower some half-mile outside the fort where a watch was kept for Indians. Jared found himself on frequent duty in this vulnerable place, and once when a large party of Indians was seen riding over a ridge, he and his companions were obliged to make a rapid retreat back down the hill to the safety of the main stockade, one man stumbling and ending up rolling over and over like a barrel.

Frequently he saw the Millard woman. Once, she met his eyes full on, then turned away and walked past him with her nose in the air. She seemed to have few friends among the other women. On another occasion, she was on the verge of speaking to him, but at that moment her husband approached and bawled at Jared to attend to the latrines.

In late June there was great jubilance at the post when a wagon train pulled in filled with immigrants; men, women and a host of children bound for the Montana goldfields. These folk brought much needed supplies, including a sawmill, and news from the outside world. Tongues babbled with excitement and three sacks of mail were produced. Jared's heart was beating fiercely as this was distributed, but as the names were called, answered, and mail was tossed to grasping hands, his hopes were sinking; then suddenly his name was called and a moment later he held an envelope. But it was not addressed in the familiar hand of Annie, but in the more stolid writing of his father. He tore it open, his hands trembling.

My Dear Jared
We have received your letters and are most thankful that you are alive and well. Sadly we cannot bring you happy news. Your dear wife Annie was smitten with the cholera and we regret to tell you that she died on . . .

Jared could read no more. His eyes blurred with tears. In the background he could hear Sergeant Millard shouting at him, but the words had no meaning in his ears. He slowly walked to his bunk in the barrack room, slumped down and was lost in his grief.

It seemed that there was now no purpose for his life.

SEVEN

A certain Captain William Jud Fetterman had arrived
at the fort. He had fine, bushy sideburns and arrogant
eyes, and after the wagon train had left under escort to
continue its journey towards Virginia City in the
north, the boast he made spread through the post.
'Give me eighty men and I will destroy the Sioux
Nation.' His superior, Colonel Carrington, was a more
cautious man and made no such boast. He restrained
Fetterman as if he were a leashed mastiff scenting
game. But soon the leash was to snap.

Jared went through the motions of his duties, but
his mind seemed numb and he felt like a prisoner in
this place. Had it not been for the oath he had given,
he would have deserted long ago and taken his chances
in the surrounding wilderness.

One August day when he was delivering some
equipment to the farrier, the wife of Sergeant Millard
passed him, carrying a basket of laundry. She looked
particularly downcast. At first he did not think she had
seen him, but suddenly she swung back and gave him
a desperate look.

'My husband,' she gasped, 'I know he treats you rough. I don't know how you stand it.'

'I don't have any option,' he said.

'You do . . . you do. You could escape from this place. I know you were an officer. You shouldn't suffer what he does to you.'

He studied her. Her hair was tumbled about her face and she looked grimy, but then he realized it wasn't dirt on her face but bruising. Instinct told him that he should not get involved with this woman, but he realized that her life must be hell.

She glanced around to make sure they were not overheard. 'I've got to get away from *him*,' she said. 'I'm his prisoner. He'll kill me. I wasn't brought up for this sort of treatment. Daddy is very rich, a senator. My mother was a famous singer, wanted me to go on the stage. But I met Horse Millard, and he looked so fine in his uniform. He proposed on bended knee, promising to keep me in the manner I was accustomed to, and I succumbed to his charms. After we married, he changed to his real self. He has such a terrible temper.' She paused to wipe tears from her eyes, then she said, 'If you escape from this place, take me with you and I'll give you everything a man wants from a woman. And my daddy will be so generous to you. I promise!'

He felt stunned by what she had said, but he knew he had to be firm.

'I won't leave this place,' he repeated, 'not until my enlistment is up.'

Her shoulders sagged. 'Think about it, Jared,' she sobbed. 'Don't say no. Think about it.'

At that moment one of the farriers came round the

corner of the building and the woman looked startled and drew away from him. Soon she was gone, stumbling under the weight of her basket.

'Best not let Horse Millard catch you talkin' to his missus,' the farrier remarked. 'He'd kill yuh.'

Jared nodded. The woman had disturbed him. She had called him by his given name. He knew he was woman-starved, just as every unmarried man was at the post. He reprimanded himself. With his dearest Annie so fresh in her grave, he had no right to allow his thoughts to dwell on another woman, particularly a married one. Even so, he felt sorry for her.

After he was discharged from the hospital for officers, Major James Shafter took a furlough, going home to his sister in Idaho. It grieved her to look at him, though she was determined not to show it. Sometimes she gazed at a photograph of him, taken at West Point. He had looked happy and immensely proud in his fine uniform, with its braid and shiny buttons. He had risen to Major quickly, having shown great courage in the early days of the Civil War. Now, she suppressed a sob. He was a wreck of a man and it hurt her eyes to see him. A deep, ghastly cicatrix, forever red and angry, distorted his forehead, there was a twitch to his eyes and his back constantly pained him. It had been a miracle that his sight had been saved, though his eyes were permanently bloodshot. She knew that his brain had been affected. Gone was the bright and considerate nature he used to have. It had been replaced by a brooding bitterness.

She had never asked him how he had sustained his

injuries, yet she knew that hatred festered inside him, and sometimes he would cry out in his sleep, tortured as he relived what had happened to him.

Yet one thing now gave him strength. The Army doctors had certified him fit for duty. Not duty in the field of battle. Maybe he could be found a nice quiet job in some military backwater. Maybe somewhere out West.

At Fort Phil Kearny the dreary months dragged by. The Indians swarmed the surrounding hills, striking as and when they could. Horses were stolen and sometimes at night warriors would sneak in close to the fort and shoot at the guards patrolling the banquettes. All the time, the post cemetery was expanding in size, as men died not only from Indian depredation, but from sickness brought on by poor diet.

It became clear that there was a good deal of discontent among the officers. Fetterman had gained much support as he bragged that an offensive should be launched against the Sioux and their villages destroyed. Colonel Carrington would have none of it and concentrated on consolidating Fort Phil Kearny. A company was dispatched northward with orders to erect a further post along the Bozeman Trail, thus providing another safe haven for travellers.

Meanwhile Jared Harris endured life, caring not overly whether he survived or not. He frequently took chances and was shot at by Indians more than once, but he was not hit, and eventually concluded that the good Lord must have plans for the remainder of his life. The thought of returning to Kentucky and not finding Annie there depressed him.

At last Christmas 1866 arrived and snow blanketed the surrounding hills. A detail had gone out to fell timber at Lodge Trail Ridge, which was out of sight from both the fort and watch-tower. But heavy gunfire was heard and it was obvious that the detail was under attack. After some brief consultation, Fetterman was dispatched to relieve the detail. Jared was standing guard at the west gate as Fetterman left the fort. He was close by as Carrington called out an order that he had given previously. *Relieve the wood detail and then come back. On no account pursue the Indians beyond Lodge Trail Ridge.*

Jared would never forget the way Fetterman turned in his saddle, gestured his acknowledgement by touching his fingers to his hat-brim. Then he swung back and Jared saw how his expression changed to exultation. *Give me eighty men and I'll ride through the Sioux Nation*, he had claimed.

Jared counted Fetterman's force as the men filed past. Was it coincidence that they numbered exactly eighty?

Those left at the fort waited apprehensively for the wood party and the relieving column to return. At last a column was seen approaching and the fort gates swung open to admit them. Sure enough it was the wood party, but not Fetterman's column. Apparently the latter had given chase to the small party of Sioux who had fled before them. Fetterman had proceeded beyond Lodge Trail Ridge despite Carrington's orders to the contrary. Presently heavy gunfire was heard and this eventually died away.

A highly alarmed Carrington dispatched a further column under Captain Ten Eyck to determine what had happened. Jared was a member of this party, and as they proceeded the weather closed in bleakly. Presently they topped a ridge and beneath them was a scene of the utmost horror. Scores of mounted Indians rode triumphantly amongst the mutilated bodies of Fetterman's slaughtered command, and now as they saw the new column they taunted Ten Eyck to charge down for further conflict. Wisely, Ten Eyck ordered his men to stand their ground, not to descend into that valley of death.

Now Jared experienced the first qualms concerning this campaign. He cursed the white greed that had forced men to enter this Indian territory, he cursed Washington's stupidity, and he cursed the savagery of the Sioux nation. But most of all he cursed the arrogant Fetterman for so blatantly disobeying his colonel's orders.

It was presently clear that the Indians were withdrawing, retreating before the ferocity of the weather, in the knowledge that they had achieved a staggering victory, having reduced Carrington's regiment by at least eighty men. Surely Fort Phil Kearny would now be easy pickings for Red Cloud and his hordes.

Ten Eyck sent back to the fort for wagons and when these were brought up he led his dejected column down into the valley and the dismal task of retrieving the dead was commenced. There were no survivors from Fetterman's command. Every body had been mutilated, scarified.

EIGHT

The garrison of Fort Phil Kearny was plunged into a state of heavy mourning, and as the blizzard gripped the land, obscuring everything in a curtain of whiteness, Jared took his turn standing guard in the freezing cold, straining his eyes for sight of the first indication that the Sioux were mounting an attack. He also worked shovelling back the snow, but it was a hapless task. Many men suffered frostbite. As snow piled up against the outside walls, it became evident that the Indians could walk straight into the fort if they chose. Against the mass of Red Cloud's warriors, the defenders would stand little chance. Men, women and children would suffer the same horrifying fate as that of Fetterman's command.

In desperation, Carrington dispatched a single volunteer, John "Portugee" Phillips, to brave the weather and the Indians who swarmed the surrounding hills. He was to ride to Fort Laramie, a distance of some 300 miles, alert the outside world to the tragedy and summon help. The chances of him getting through seemed slim – but his ride was to become one of the legends of the West, a tremendous feat of courage and endurance. The Indians never attacked the fort and a week later the relieving force arrived, bringing welcome reinforcements. The dejected garrison was thus saved.

But, as well as the Indian threat, Jared Harris had other problems on his hands. As the passing weeks brought a departure of the snows and the first sign of spring, with the surrounding hills showing green, more timber was brought in to strengthen the walls of the fort, and one day as he was working with an axe, splitting pine-trunks into logs, he felt a presence behind him, and, turning, he saw the woman, Sergeant Millard's wife. She looked more forlorn than ever.

'Jared Harris,' she said. 'I need help desperately. Like I said, my daddy will be so grateful. He's a surgeon, a wonderful man, who just wants me home so bad. You're the only person I can turn to . . .'

'I thought you said he was a senator,' he said.

'Yes . . . that too.'

Impatience flared in Jared. 'Now look here, Mrs Millard . . .'

'Call me Jessie,' she cut in. 'Having *his* name makes me shudder.'

'If he finds out you're speaking to me, he'll murder us both. Can't you see that?'

'Not if we get away,' she said. 'Now the weather has changed, we could take our chances up the Bozeman Trail. Maybe we could get through to Virginia City and start a new life. Surely you want that as much as I do.'

He shook his head. He did not know what to say, but he felt that every second she delayed with him, the greater danger they were in. He was not physically afraid of Millard. He could stand his abuse, his unfair treatment . . . but he was afraid of the trouble he could bring.

'I should never have married him,' she said. 'I didn't realize what a brute of a man he was, and I didn't know he already had a wife.'

Jared gasped in surprise. 'You mean he's a bigamist!'

She nodded, tears glistening in her eyes. 'For God's sake help me escape. I can't get away by myself.'

'No, Mrs Millard,' he said. 'I will finish my enlistment with the army. I have given my word.'

Anger showed in her big eyes. 'You'll regret it,' she said. 'He hates you, Jared Harris, even worse than any other Rebel. He hates you because you're cleverer than he is. Mark my words, he'll get you killed one way or another.'

Jared turned his back on her, took his annoyance out on the log he was chopping. Eventually, when he swung back, she was gone.

James Shafter was a changed man, but recovery from his awesome wounds was hastened by the bitterness that brewed inside him, and the desire to resume his military career. With sad eyes, his sister nursed him back to a level of health beyond which he would never go. He avoided mirrors at all costs because the sight of himself made him shudder – the gorgonian scar, like a jagged canyon across the top of his forehead which seemed to draw the skin of his face to tautness, as if it were a bag twisted at the top. Severe headaches remained to torment him. At night he lay awake for hours, his festering thoughts replaced by equally grim nightmares when sleep at last came.

The days passed, and at last the doctors informed him that he could return to duty, albeit in some western backwater where the demands would not be so great. He willingly put on his uniform, but now he wore his hat whenever possible, pulling it down to hide the hideousness of the scar.

But Fate had dealt yet another strange blow, for he was headed for a place that was anything but a 'peaceful' backwater, and where events were to fuel his bitter hatred and push him further along his path of vengeance.

While convalescing, Shafter had read in the newspapers of the tragic events at the Western outpost. How some eighty soldiers had been overwhelmed by Sioux Indians. He also read of the recriminations that had been heaped on the commanding officer, Colonel Carrington, who, it was claimed, should never have allowed the disaster to happen. The nation needed a scapegoat, and the result was that Carrington was relieved of his command.

When James Shafter travelled to Fort Phil Kearny by wagon train, he had as his companion Carrington's replacement, Colonel Wessells. It was now well into autumn and the trails were already streaked with snow. By the time they arrived, Carrington and his wife had left.

Shafter was appointed commander of C Company, his predecessor having been bedded down to recover from painful piles which had rendered him unable to sit in his saddle.

As Shafter checked through the company lists on his first day at work, two matters quickened his interest. The first was that serving at the post was a certain Sergeant Horse Millard, who had been his subordinate at Shiloh and had subsequently been charged with drunkenness and transferred from the regiment.

The second was that one of the privates in B Company was a 'Galvanized Yankee' and had been an officer in the Confederate Army. Shafter decided to find out more about this man.

'I hear you been pestering my wife!'

The angry words stung Jared as he unsaddled his sorrel in the stable. He and a dozen others had just returned from patrol. He turned and saw the heavy-shouldered figure of Sergeant Horse Millard blocking the light through the stable doorway.

One of the privates standing near to Jared, a man who was always fawning up to the sergeant, said, 'Yeah, Sarge, I heard that too. 'Bout time you taught that Rebel a damned lesson.'

Jared didn't respond. He met Millard's hateful glare. The non-com's face was boiling with rage, twice as red as normal. It was clear he had been drinking. Jared felt a wave of compassion for Jessie Millard.

'Deny it,' he spat at Jared, 'and I'll call you a liar!'

'I do deny it,' Jared said coolly.

'Damn you!' Millard snarled, and he unbuckled his tunic, drew it off and cast it down into the straw. His paunch sagged over the belt of his trousers. 'I'll teach you a lesson, Harris. You'll never touch her again after

this. Strip off. You can forget I'm a sergeant. We'll see
who's the best man!'

And suddenly, the other men were drawing around,
forming a ring in the stable. This was not the first time
Millard had taught one of his subordinates a lesson,
nigh beating him to death, another one for his list.

Jared felt his own anger rising. He unbuttoned his
tunic and, forcing himself to remain calm, removed it,
folded it and placed it down, sensing the sergeant's
impatience growing. Many times he had longed to take
a swipe at this brutish man, but he had restrained
himself for obvious reasons. Now his chance had come.
Even so he felt that in responding to the man's
violence, he might be playing into his hands, laying
himself open for any number of bad repercussions. But
there was no time for further thoughts. Millard took a
striding, squatty leap, feinting with his left fist, catching Jared a glancing blow across the jaw with his right,
sending him staggering back to the jeering laughter of
those watching.

Jared forced himself up, wiping his jaw with the
back of his hand, seeing a smear of blood. He realized
that Millard was wearing some sort of knuckleduster,
his fingers ringed by hard metal.

Various images bombarded Jared's mind – the old
hatred for Yankees, the vision of Jessie's Millard's sad
face. And his own fury suddenly erupted and he flew at
Millard, cleaving the air with wild swings of his fists.
Millard dodged back, luring Jared on, grunting with
delight at the way his opponent had risen to his bait.
The two men both lunged at the same time, their
bodies thudding together, their eyes scant inches

apart. Millard brought his knee up with crunching force, catching Jared in the crotch, sending tears of agony lancing across his vision. He was cast aside, doubled over with pain, hearing Millard's cry of triumph. He landed on all fours, dodging to the left as Millard swung his booted foot in a vicious kick. But before his adversary could regain his balance, Jared grabbed his foot, twisted it, hanging on like a leech. It was Millard's turn to come tumbling down into the straw. Jared dragged himself on top of the sergeant, finding room to swing his fists. He pummelled his adversary about the face, feeling his teeth splinter under his knuckles. With a growl of animal fury, Millard flung him aside, catching him across the cheek with his knuckleduster. A half-inch closer and it would have gouged Jared's eye. As it was, the blow split his cheek open. Both men were now covered in blood, their mouths lolling as they sucked in air.

Millard, crouched low, head-butted for the stomach, but Jared twisted his hips. Even so Millard reared to grasp him by the throat, his grip tightening, Jared's eyes bulging as he fought for breath. He could hear the mob shrieking at their sergeant. 'Squeeze the shit out o' him, Sarge! Finish him off!'

Jared was almost done, the unrelenting grip of the New Yorker throttling him, everything around going a throbbing green. In desperation he rammed his knee upward into Millard's crotch, and luck favoured him. Millard unleashed an agonized roar, his grip slackening. Jared shrugged himself free, in no mood for mercy. He ploughed in with all his strength, sensing that this was his last chance. He caught Millard a savage punch in the kidneys, then his right fist came surging up almost from his boots, connecting solidly with the sergeant's jaw, and he knew the fight was over.

Millard was sprawled on his back, half-buried in straw, his face a bloody pulp.

For a moment the watching throng seemed stunned into silence, hardly believing what they had seen.

'My God,' somebody at last gasped, 'he's knocked Sarge out cold!'

'He'll pay for it, sure as Texas!'

'Never thought I'd see the day.'

The mob moved back, almost respectfully, as Jared, gathering up his tunic, shouldered his way unsteadily through. A moment later he was at the sluice, washing the blood from his battered body. He feared that when he had knocked Millard out he had broken his wrist, but now he probed it with his other hand he felt reasonably sure it was merely bruised. He grinned to himself. He wondered if he had broken Millard's jaw. Whether he had or not, the sergeant was not going to be a happy man when he regained his senses, and he was not the type to take a drubbing without getting his revenge. Jared hoped he would not take it out on his wife. One thing was certain. The sergeant was unlikely to let matters rest.

NINE

It was a week later. Major Shafter had spoken to Sergeant Millard's company commander and broached the possibility of a transfer of the non-com to C Company. 'As you know,' Shafter said, the side of his face affected by what seemed a permanent twitch, 'I served with Millard in the war. We're due for Wagon Box duty next week and I'd like him with me.'

The Wagon Box camp was some six miles south-west of Forth Phil Kearny, a base where guards were stationed to protect civilian contractors who were employed to cut timber for the army. It was somewhat isolated, but there had been no sign of Indians since the Fetterman disaster, and the general hope was that they had returned to the Black Hills area.

Major Ten Eyck scratched his nose. He knew that Millard had got himself severely thrashed in a fist-fight and was still recovering. Ten Eyck did not favour such behaviour from his non-coms. The New Yorker had created a lot of trouble since he had been in B Company, with his drinking, his pathetic wife and his harsh ways.

'I'll agree a transfer,' he said a little too eagerly, 'provided I can get an adequate replacement.'

Shafter smiled his lopsided smile. 'I'll make sure you do. I'll speak to Wessells.'

Next day, Millard reported to Shafter's office. After he had saluted, Shafter rose from behind his desk, shook his hand. Each man noted the other's injuries, but neither commented. It was a touchy and sensitive subject.

'It'll be a pleasure to serve with you, sir,' Millard remarked. 'Bring back memories of the old days.'

'You've probably heard we're due for the Wagon Box camp. Things should be pretty quiet out there. The Indians seemed to have left this country.'

'About time too,' Millard said, and then he frowned.

'What's wrong, Sergeant?'

'It's a question of my wife, sir. I had to – eh – reprimand a certain individual for pestering her. I wouldn't fancy leaving her unprotected while I'm away.'

'Certainly not,' Shafter said. 'Who is this individual?'

'A Private Jared Harris, sir. He's a Galvanized Yankee. He was an officer – in fact, the captain of the Eighth Kentucky at Shiloh and Gettysburg.'

'Eighth Kentucky!' Shafter's back had stiffened, his eyes suddenly twitching with excitement. Some trigger in his memory had been squeezed, a vision of a flag fluttering in his mind.

He said, 'I'll make arrangements to have him watched while we're away.'

'I was wondering, sir, if he might be transferred to this company. He'd be out of harm's way at the Wagon Box camp, and I'd keep an eye on him myself.'

Shafter was breathing heavily. An idea settled into his mind. He made a distinct effort to calm himself 'Yes, Sergeant,' he said, feigning indifference. 'I'll see if I can get him transferred over to us.'

'Thank you, sir.' Millard's battered features cracked into a smile. As he left the office, his thoughts were racing ahead. The tour of duty out at the Wagon Box camp lasted a month. Anything could happen out there, away from the watching eyes at Fort Phil Kearny. And after all, the Indians could always be blamed if a man was found with a bullet in his back, particularly if his scalp was torn off.

The following Tuesday, Jared was part of the detachment that marched south of the Sullivant Hills along the wood road and through the forest towards the Wagon Box camp. At first, he had welcomed his transfer to C Company, but his heart had sunk when he realized that Millard had also been transferred. Shafter's command consisted of thirty men, all armed with new Springfield-Allen repeating rifles, the so-called 'needle guns'.

Sergeant Millard appeared to have recovered from the battering he had taken, his normal bullying manner having reasserted itself, but he showed Jared no particular attention and avoided his eye. This day was stifling and along the forest trail they encountered a silence that seemed almost reproachful. There had been little sign of Indians since the Fetterman débâcle six months earlier, and on arrival at the camp, the present incumbents welcomed them as a break from their crushing month-long boredom. 'Deadlier than a

Sunday-school picnic,' one man remarked.

The camp lay on cleared ground some hundred yards up slope from the Little Piney stream and beyond this tall pines curtained off the view. The camp consisted of an oval-shaped corral, enclosed by fourteen wagon-boxes, the wheels having been removed. The wood-choppers' camp was 1,200 yards to the south.

Within a couple of hours, the change-over had been completed, and the relieved command had marched out on their return trip to Fort Phil Kearny.

During the afternoon of that first day, C Company commenced settling in, stacking supplies, cleaning weapons, checking ammunition. The cooks set up their stoves and started to prepare food. Scouts were sent out, but reported back that there was no sign of hostiles.

Jared felt Millard's eyes on him, but whenever he turned the sergeant was looking elsewhere. Even so, he didn't trust the man, particularly when his back was turned. Millard would never forget the drubbing he had taken. Jared sensed he was just waiting his chance to get his revenge. He wondered who had told Millard that he had conversed with his wife, and to what extent the story had been embroidered to give the impression that he had 'pestered' her, or was that interpretation of Millard's making? Which ever way it was, he had little doubt that Millard would have punished Jessie in some brutal fashion.

For the first time, Jared had the opportunity to study Major Shafter. The officer was tall and angular, his pale face often twisted in a grimace as if he suffered constant pain. Whatever he did, he wore his hat pulled well down, and Jared heard that this was because he had a bad scar, sustained during the war. Nonetheless, he appeared to go about his duties in a quiet and efficient manner. He seemed far too busy to pay attention to the lowly private under his command, despite the fact that he was a Galvanized Yankee.

The evening meal was served, men lining up holding their tin plates. Jared drank his coffee, finding it somewhat bitter, but dismissed it as of no importance. He felt weary, having worked hard, and would gladly have taken to his blankets, but from the duty roster, he learned that Millard had given him the first stint of picket duty. As always, he obeyed orders without complaint, and took up position on the far side of the stream, at a point which offered a slightly elevated view and at which somebody had erected a shelter of willows with a poncho fixed over. As darkness filtered through the trees, his tiredness increased and he felt his eyelids dropping. He fought against it. He remembered his coffee. Was it possible that somebody had slipped something into it? Was this Millard's way of getting back at him? He tried to rule out the idea, but the overwhelming desire to doze was getting worse. He had never felt this way when on duty before.

An hour later a corporal discovered him fast asleep at his post.

When he was hauled before Major Shafter the following morning on a formal charge of sleeping while on guard duty, the stern-faced officer showed no compassion, taking no notice of the fact that Jared still seemed unsteady on his feet.

'You have placed your comrades at risk,' he snapped. 'You could have had us all killed, Private Harris. Tomorrow, you will be escorted back to the fort. There, you will stand trial for this grave offence. Meanwhile, in the absence of a guard-room here, you are to be chained to a wagon-wheel.'

Jared took this judgment without comment. He knew nobody would believe any story about his coffee being doctored.

At noon the sun beat down upon his head unmercifully. He had lost his hat, and, in his position, shackled tightly to the spokes of a wagon-wheel, there was no shade. Flies buzzed about him incessantly and his only defence against them was a shake of his head. Each time he slipped into a doze, he awoke to find them caked on his sweating face.

For the past months he had suffered the resentment of his fellows, a resentment that was intensified each time he spoke in the Southern voice he could not disguise. The war lived on in men's hearts, even in his own, though he took great care to conceal it. The fact that he had always kept to himself and did not indulge in the crude profanity of the others, rendered him an oddity. So now he neither expected nor received the slightest mercy.

One of Sergeant Millard's lackeys, a Private Grady, sat a few yards away, having found himself a shady spot and considering himself lucky to have landed the job of guarding the ex-Confederate. Certainly sitting in the shade was better than chopping timber or running errands for Millard. He knew that Harris was desperate for water and he took a delight in positioning the canteen just a few inches beyond his reach. Private Grady roused himself late in the afternoon, unlocked Jared's handcuff and escorted him to the latrines, keeping his rifle aimed at him all the time. He laughed as Jared stumbled on his stiff legs and said, 'One crazy trick from you, and I'll blow your damned head off. Those are Sergeant Millard's orders.'

'Don't worry,' Jared growled. 'I'll not give you that satisfaction,' and beneath his breath, he added, 'Not yet. Not yet!'

He knew his situation was desperate. Sleeping on duty was a grave offence. Men had been shot for less, and he suspected that any punishment inflicted on him back at Fort Phil Kearny would be harsh and quick. He had heard that he would be returned to the fort the following day. He wondered if some opportunity of escape would present itself during the journey. It was a forlorn hope, but it was all he had to cling to as he was escorted back to the wagon-wheel and his handcuff refastened.

That night he watched the moon come up, studied the remote twinkling of stars, and heard the coyotes and owls call from the forest. He envied them their freedom. Picket guards came and went and cramp tormented him. He was still awake when the drummer beat reveille.

TEN

After breakfast and roll-call, Major James Shafter decided to take a bath in the stream some one hundred yards from the encampment. He and his young lieutenant, John Jenness, left the circle of the camp and walked to the stream. Here, they stripped off and immersed themselves in the water. As was his custom, Shafter kept his hat on. His headache was particularly bad. He sometimes imagined that his brains were like jagged rocks, grinding against each other inside his skull. Now the cool, cleansing feel of the stream brought him slight relief, and he allowed himself a rare smile.

He had done a little probing into the background of Private Jared Harris, examining official documents back at the fort. What he had discovered had hardened his resolve. Without doubt this was the man he wanted dead, and it seemed that Fate had dealt him the chance he had longed for. Sergeant Millard's accusations of wife-molesting against the Southerner had made matters even simpler. Millard's hatred was as intense as his own, though for very different reasons.

However, Shafter had to be careful. He had ample evidence to have Harris executed, but others would carry out the task so that he would not be implicated. But before Harris died, he would enlighten him to the fact that his punishment was not only for sleeping on duty, but for other wicked deeds that he had committed.

Suddenly both officers were alarmed by the raucous cries of crows in the trees to their left and two shots blasted off. Almost simultaneously a man who had been standing guard pointed wildly and shouted, 'Injuns comin'!' and he ran headlong back towards the camp. It was then that the blood-curdling cacophony of Indian warcries sounded desperately close at hand.

Shafter and young Jenness were out of the stream in haste, not stopping to collect their clothes as they sprinted for the cover of the encampment. Shafter's hat was wafted from his head. As he turned to recover it, he glimpsed the horrifying sight of Indians swarming from the forest beyond the stream. They were mostly naked, their bodies painted white, green and yellow, which made them look like hideous devils. They were driving their ponies back and forth, waving their guns, Spencer carbines snatched from Captain Fetterman's butchered command, their whooping and yelling full of defiance, their intention clearly to repeat the massacre of seven months ago. *My God*, Shafter thought, *there's thousands of them!* He raced on, following Jenness through a gap between the wagon-boxes.

The Indians surged up from the stream, circling around to cut the encampment off from the fort.

As Shafter pulled on some clothing, his face

reflected a desperate do-or-die expression. But there was something else too. A look of strange exultation.

'Remember Fetterman!' he shouted. 'Shoot to kill!' and he ordered ammunition boxes opened, his men to take up position behind the wagon-boxes and open fire. They were fighting for their lives and needed no second invitation.

Looking beyond the barricade, Shafter felt he had never seen so many hostiles before, and they were all mounted, chanting war- and death-songs. He was aware that the camp was truly isolated. In the valley of the Little Piney, more warriors were assembling. Suddenly the encircling attackers surged forward from the south and Shafter cried out, 'Men, here they come. Take your places and make every shot count!' He was to give no further orders. None was necessary.

Jared Harris writhed against his shackling handcuff, cursing his helplessness. If the Indians surged over the barricade, he would have no means of defending himself. Many of the defenders knew the score well and if they were overwhelmed would turn their guns upon themselves rather than submit to the inevitable torture inflicted on prisoners. For Jared there would be no such luxury. Utter pandemonium reigned. The gunfire became deafening, the warcries of the Indians horrendous as arrows and bullets pounded into the barricades, the wood of the wagon-beds becoming splintered. As their ammunition ran out, men would crawl on their hands and knees, ducking furtively, to collect more shells from the big green boxes.

Jared was aware of the deadly *thrum* of arrows, and the thud as they hit the covering wagons. Soon the

Indians had elevated their aim, sending their missiles skyward so that they plunged down within the corral. Somehow the prospect of being pinned by an arrow was more awful than the threat of a bullet.

Shafter knew that his command was hopelessly outnumbered, and as casualties began to be sustained, he realized that every gun counted. His gaze swung to Private Harris still chained to the wagonwheel and he turned to the corporal standing next to him and ordered that the Southerner be released, given a rifle and placed at the southern side of the camp. The prospects of him running off were nil.

Jared grunted with relief as he was set free, working his cramped limbs to restore the circulation. With stiff, trembling fingers, he rammed shells into the breech of his restored Springfield and gathered up his bayonet. A moment later he had taken up position at the barricade alongside the other tight-jawed defenders. From behind, he heard the voice of Sergeant Millard bawling orders. The view before him was totally daunting. Through an irregular line of contractors' tents which somehow still remained erect, he could see that Indians were circling around, gradually drawing in closer, brandishing war clubs and tomahawks, and others still more daring would ride almost up to the barricade, then suddenly drop to the offside of their mounts, discharging their muskets from beneath the bellies of their animals.

The warriors would brave the first blast of gunfire, some going down. The survivors would then come in even closer, and Jared realized that they were unaware that the soldiers possessed repeating rifles, believing that the old ramrod-loading muskets were still in use. Instead, the defenders were able to throw open their breech blocks, eject empty shells, reload and continue firing. And suddenly the Indians were drawing back to a safe distance, leaving the ground strewn with the dead and dying. And now came a lull in the firing.

Jared sensed that the Indians would not be daunted. They had come to inflict another massacre upon the hated bluecoats and they would be prepared for sacrifice. Soon he could see them re-forming in readiness for a fresh onslaught, signalling with mirrors as if to bring up reinforcements.

Nearly all the soldiers were bare-headed, using their hats to hold ammunition, and the sun burned down upon them in a pitiless glare. Suddenly somebody shouted, 'Look out, they're comin' again!' and Jared gazed out to see Indians to the south-east urging their ponies forward for another attack. He realized why the Indians had allowed the tents to remain. They concealed their movements from the soldiers, and men now cursed that the canvas had not been dismantled.

'Too late to take 'em down now,' somebody gasped. 'It'd be suicide to go out there.'

Sergeant Millard had other ideas. He called out the names of four men . . . 'Smith, Galliard, Webber . . . and Harris. Get out there. Get them tents pulled down.'

'Sarge, we can't . . .' Webber started, but Millard bawled him into silence.

Jared felt the familiar tightening of his chest as his lungs constricted with fear, but came to his feet along with the reluctant others. They checked their Springfields, glanced anxiously at the sergeant as if hoping he would change his mind, but his expression remained fixed. Jared was first to move between the wagon boxes into the dangerous world beyond. The others followed, relying on his big frame to shield them. Their view of the Indians and the ground in between was obscured by the four tents, the nearest of which was some thirty feet from the barricade, but there was no doubting the close proximity of their enemies, for the ground was shuddering with the thunder of approaching hoofs. Sporadic fire had commenced from the soldiers behind the wagon boxes. This should have provided comfort, but Jared didn't like having his back turned on men who had only a narrow gap through which to fire between the obstructing tents. Some shots were whining unpleasantly close.

Jared freed his bayonet and the others followed suit. They tackled the nearest of the tents, slashing the guy-ropes and having it collapsing about the supply boxes of contractors' tools which it contained. The roar of gunfire was intensifying as they rushed forward to the second tent, their view of the Indians still obscured. With frenzied hands, they brought the canvas down. Jared glanced around at his companions. Their faces were pallid and tight-lipped with fear, their eyes showing panic.

'Let's go back now,' Private Webber, little more than a boy, cried. 'We done all we can!'

And it was at that moment that Private Galliard, standing close to Jared, let out a shocked gasp of pain and dropped to the ground, lying face down. Jared glanced at his motionless body, half stooped to help him up, then saw the bullet hole in his back oozing blood. Simultaneously another bullet whined, splintering a tent-pole scant inches away. He risked a look behind him, saw guns poking from the wagon-boxes and sensed instantly that the bullet had been intended for him, most likely from Millard's gun.

Arrows were thrumming over their heads, plunging into the wood of the wagon-boxes. Smith and Webber had had enough; they had both started back towards the barricade. Jared was in two minds whether to follow them, but the prospect of being shot down by Millard convinced him that there was as much danger at his rear as there was to his front. He staggered on towards the third tent, but now he got a glimpse of approaching horsemen, their bodies adorned with streaming feathers and daubed with hideous painted designs. It was too late to dismantle the canvas of the last tent, too late even to turn back. In desperation he lunged through the flap of the tent, hoping to find some shielding supply boxes. There was nothing!

Pandemonium was reigning beyond the canvas, as the shrieking Indians swept past, the blast of muskets, and the pound of hoofs clamorous. The tent shuddered as something blundered against its guy-rope. A bullet sliced through the canvas close to Jared. He stood, rifle in one hand, naked bayonet in the other, expecting to die at any moment. As if in fulfilment of his expectations, the tent flap was ripped aside, and an Indian warrior in a war bonnet appeared, his frenzied expression changing to one of exultation as he confronted Jared. Immediately he lunged forward, his tomahawk raised to brain the Kentuckian, but Jared was no stranger to hand-to-hand fighting and he ducked aside, slashing at the Indian with the bayonet. The warrior grunted with the fanatical joy of combat. Within the tent there was little room for manoeuvre. The two men closed, grappling with each other, the bear-grease stench of the Indian mingling with that of gunpowder and gritty dust. Both were slippery with sweat, but Jared was at a disadvantage because the Indian gripped his tunic and swung his tomahawk again. But it never fell. Jed jabbed his bayonet up in desperation, felt it slice into his adversary's belly and blood gush over his hand. The Indian staggered back, his face contorted in agony. He sank to his knees, his lips moving as he launched into his death chant, then that gurgled to nothingness and he fell forward on his face.

Again the tent was shuddering as ponies blundered against the guy-ropes. Jared glanced at the fallen Indian, seeing his splendid war bonnet. He knew that at any moment more Indians were bound to burst in. Desperately, he grappled with the buttons of his tunic and pulled it off, together with his undershirt. He stooped down, gathered up the war bonnet and put it on his own head. He was rising again when a further idea came to him and he knelt down once more, thrust his fingers into the blood from the man's ripped gut and spread it across his own bare torso. He knew his appearance would not stand close inspection, but the casual observer might be tricked. It was his only chance.

Gritting his teeth, he pushed his way out of the tent, praying that luck was with him. The air was thick with dust and gunsmoke, but there seemed a slight lessening of the firing. He gasped as he saw bodies covering the ground – Indian bodies, ponies' hulks. Some of them were trying to rise. Glancing ahead, the fear was in him that the Indians, despite staggering losses, had won the day, had overwhelmed the defenders of the wagon-boxes, but through the thick air, the barricade still appeared intact, and as he stood, somebody took a shot at him, sending lead plucking at his head-dress. This time he sensed that it was not personal hatred that motivated the marksman, but the effectiveness of his disguise. He realized that corpses and the dying were not his only companions. Indian warriors were still close at hand, some of them even glancing in his direction but seemingly dismissing him as one of their own.

Suddenly, movement to his left caught his attention. An Indian, obviously weakened by a wound, was striving to remount his pony. Knowing that now was no time for compassion, Jared thrust the bayonet into his belt, reversed the Springfield in his blood-slippery hands. He charged at the struggling Indian and clouted him against the side of the head with a wild swing of his rifle butt. The Indian dropped like a stone without uttering a cry. The paint-daubed pony reared in panic, but Jared, losing his grip on the Springfield, got hold of the rope-reins and somehow dragged himself up astride the pad saddle. He glanced around, grunting with relief. Nobody appeared to be paying him much attention. Indian riders were moving amongst their fallen comrades, some of whom were clambering to their feet to be lifted up behind their rescuers. The slaughter had been immense.

Within seconds, Jared was heeling his pony forward, hugging himself low against the animal's back, controlling it with its simple rope bridle. Initially, he followed mounted Indians as they retired from the battlefield. But he had no desire for company, not from Redskins nor his own kind. Particularly as the only weapon he had left was an overworked, bloodstained bayonet.

He dragged on the reins, veering the pony off to the side, the tail feathers of the war bonnet streaming behind him, praying aloud that he could find cover in the forest before somebody tumbled to his ruse.

ELEVEN

Panic motivated the pony's gallop as much as Jared's thumping heels. Not until they had splashed across the stream and reached the fringe of pine-forest, did he rein in the heaving animal and swing round to contemplate the scene behind him. Smeared with blood, sweating, his chest bared, the war bonnet now askew on his head, he grappled to get his breath under control. The sight before him resembled the Civil War carnage, for the ground was strewn with the dead and wounded.

It was clear that the Sioux had attacked the encampment in great numbers, anticipating another victory, but the outcome had come as a shock in the form of the Springfield Allen repeaters and their continuous, accurate fire. At first this had not deterred the onslaught; instead it appeared to have stung the Indians into increased fanaticism. They had hurled themselves at the barricade, their numbers being decimated by the deadly fire. But now they had realized that the day was not be theirs. All they could do was gather up their casualties, despite the desultory fire that still came from the defenders, and retire to their villages wherever they were. Tonight there would be a great weeping and wailing around camp-fires as losses were counted.

For the moment, Jared felt strangely detached from events. He watched the Indians recovering the dead and dying, until eventually all that remained were the hulks of horses, some of which were still threshing. Again the prospect of returning to the barricaded camp occurred to Jared, but he dismissed it. The charge of sleeping on duty was grave, and to return would be stupidity. A slim chance of survival had now come his way and he knew he must brave this hostile, Indian-infested wilderness. But of course in doing so he was incurring yet another serious charge – that of desertion. He consoled himself with the thought he could only face a firing squad once.

He discarded his feathered head-dress, and kicked his pony into motion, riding deeper into the forest and away from the army encampment, constantly keeping a wary eye open for Indians. The last thing he wanted was to blunder into them. He knew that if he gave the pony its head, it was liable to gallop back towards familiar encampments or villages, so he held the animal in tight rein, heading, so far as he could ascertain, in a northward direction.

As he rode, he encountered no other sign of life apart from the scurryings of wild creatures. He wondered what conditions were like within the Wagon Box camp. Had heavy casualties been sustained among the soldiers? And now his conscience pricked him. Perhaps he did owe something to the Army, despite the shoddy way he had been treated. The thought that men might be suffering and dying without proper medical care within the stockade troubled him. Even worse, the Indians might be planning another attack. Perhaps he had one more duty to perform before he turned away from his military commitments. He must carry word of what had happened to Fort Phil Kearny. There, they would still be unaware of his crimes. Thereafter he would escape to whatever Fate held in store for him.

So he swung his pony back over familiar ground towards the fort, shutting his mind to the craziness of what he was doing. But he had covered only half the distance when, topping a rise, he saw a familiar column of blue beneath him and knew that he had been spared his task. This was clearly a relief force, heading for the encampment, and they had several howitzers trundling along behind. He recalled that a number of civilian contractors had fled. They must have carried word of the attack.

Once again he changed direction, heading northward. Vague thoughts of the Bozeman Trail, the famed Alder Gulch and far-off Virginia City drifted into his mind as he rode. Up there, he knew, were the goldfields. Despite the obvious dangers these offered, he still longed to return to some semblance of civilization – albeit, the lawless world of prospectors greedily scouring the land for rapid wealth, and those who attempted to exploit them. There, he decided, he might find the obscurity that he so desperately needed. Maybe he could lie low for a month or so and then. . . ? He did not know. Certainly the ruins of his home in far-off Kentucky offered him little now that he was a widower. All he could do was take his chances and be thankful for that.

Major James Shafter and his embattled defenders viewed the approaching army column with a cheer. Shafter had become exulted during the fight, shirking cover to direct fire at the Indian hordes, thrilled by the devastating casualties that the Springfield Allens had inflicted. Losses among the soldiers had been incredibly light, despite the flimsiness of their cover. He took great pride in the fact that not one Indian had breached their defences. Even so, he inwardly fumed with rage when he learned that his arrested 'Galvanized Yankee' had somehow escaped. He viewed it as a grave mis-handling of affairs and blamed himself. The escape of a prisoner would not reflect well on his record. He concluded that Millard had proved himself to be a bungling fool.

Millard had clearly believed that stepping outside the barricades to collapse the tents offered no alternative but death, but somehow the man had eluded bullets, Indians and the overwhelming odds against survival, for his body had not been recovered. He wondered if the Indians had carried the Southerner's body away, but he dismissed the idea. His scalp, possibly, but there would have been no reason to remove his body when they were so busy recovering the bodies of their own wounded. The only conclusion was that the man had somehow escaped. Just at the time when he was being congratulated on his leadership and success against the Indians, the Southerner's escape was the one blot on his copy-book. Of course if the circumstances had been different, it might have been possible to hush the business up, but the whole detachment had been aware of Harris's arrest and detention and speculation about his fate was one of the talking-points amongst the men.

Sergeant Millard was shame-faced about the incident and thereafter kept a low profile, being merely a shadow of his old self. Yet he did not take Shafter's dressing down lightly. It fanned the hatred that already existed in his heart, fanned it to a bitter intensity that would only be satisfied when Harris was dead. And with his army enlistment due to run out in six months, he decided to bide his time, take the gratuity that was due to him and then track the man down.

The relief force remained at the Wagon Box camp for two days and then, with all sign of the Indians vanished, returned to Fort Phil Kearny. Major Shafter's detachment settled down to complete the remainder of its tour of duty, during which it experienced no further attacks and was able to send a good supply of timber back to the fort for construction work.

But Major Shafter knew little satisfaction, even when the press subsequently acclaimed his gallantry and painted him as one of the Nation's great heroes. Instead, his health deteriorated by the day, the pain in his head and back driving him crazy. But worse was the bitter resentment that smouldered inside him.

TWELVE

Jared Harris spent three days and nights in the vicinity, hiding himself in the shadows of the pine-forest and being ever alert for either soldiers or Indians. Once, jarring any thoughts that he was safe, he saw against the blue sky puffs of white smoke rising from the foothills of the Bighorns to the west, and prayed that there was no reference to him in that smoke-talk. He subsisted on berries that he hoped were edible but was not certain, and later he managed to stun a trout in a stream with a rock. He laboured for a long hour whittling away with a stick until he sparked some twigs into flame. He then cooked his meal and had never tasted anything more delicious. Next day he made himself a primitive bow and arrow and thereafter knew he would not starve. The woods were alive with game.

He spent two nights in caves, and one in the uprooted bole of a tree felled by lightning. The nights were cool and he was glad of the Indian blanket which had been on the pony's back. He had never been so alone in all his life, and he suspected that he had no friends between here and far-off Kentucky. Furthermore, he had not a cent in the world, at least not where he could get at it. When he rested, he hobbled the pony's front legs, or left it securely tethered to trees. He knew that long and perilous miles, maybe three hundred, lay between him and civilization, and he could not risk having the pony run off.

On the fourth day, he crossed the Bozeman Trail – a wide expanse that had been blazed by the explorer John Bozeman as a short cut for travellers to make their way to the goldfields. Along its track, he discovered evidence of cattle herds and of wagon trains that had passed this way. Wheel-ruts; cooking stoves and pots which had been abandoned to lighten the load; the skeletons of horses and cattle which had succumbed to the hardships of the journey; the ashes of old camp-fires – and even a number of graves, indicated with crosses. Most marked the burial spots of young children and bore simple and heart-touching epitaphs.

He studied the trail for evidence of the recent passage of a wagon train, one that he might overtake and join, but he found nothing to encourage him. All sign on the trail was old, the ravages of the Sioux and the scarcity of military escorts having kept travellers to a minimum.

He edged away from the trail, climbing the lower slopes of the Bighorn Mountains, finding concealment in the pines. Far above the timber belt, the peaks towered, snow-tipped and formidable. He had no wish to go close to Fort Phil Kearny or Fort C.F. Smith, so he paralleled the trail as it ran north, crossing arroyos and canyons, knowing it would eventually lead him to Virginia City. Once he reached Montana Territory, he

would be safer. This was Crow country and they were
enemies of the Sioux and friendly to whites. But he had
a long way to travel and there was no guarantee that
he would survive the rigours of the wild. The Fall was
approaching, and soon winds would howl down from
the north; silent, deepening snow would come, and
temperatures would plummet.

He travelled for a week, conscious that the days
were growing shorter, forever wary, keeping out of
sight as much as possible. Three times he sighted
Indians upon the trail and climbed higher into the
thick, brooding forest. On another occasion, with the
purple shadows of dusk cloaking the mountains, he
almost rode into a Sioux village, but was alerted at the
last moment by the barking of dogs. Looking ahead he
glimpsed the forked poles of tipis. He rapidly back-
tracked and rode in a wide circle. He had now developed a fear of Indians that he sensed he would never
lose. Many times he was alerted by the sound of movement in the trees, and he would rein in, only to
discover that it came from wildlife – deer, moose, wood-
land bison, wild turkey and black bears.

He forded several rivers, among which, he guessed,
were the Tongue and Bighorns. His diet consisted
mainly of rabbit and squirrel and his skill with the bow
and creating fire grew. He drank from the fresh, clear
streams. The pony grazed on the lush patches of grass.
He had long since washed the Indian paint from its
flanks and once he got a decent saddle and shoes,
nobody would know the animal had once been an
Indian mount, apart from its preference for being
mounted from the right.

In the third week, he smelt smoke on the air; he tethered his pony and crept in close to where a camp was. A few rough-looking characters were sitting around a fire and such was their appearance that he felt a hasty retreat would be better than establishing a relationship. These men were outlaws and would offer him little hospitality beyond a hail of bullets.

Next morning the sound of guttural voices awakened him. Alarmed, he opened his eyes. A couple of yards away, two Indians stood gazing at him, their faces like granite, their bronzed bodies naked apart from hair-pipe breastplates and breech-cloths. They both held rifles. He sat up, feeling sickened. He met their stare, then he said, 'Virginia City,' hoping they could speak English. Whether they could he never knew, but one of them pointed to the Bozeman Trail and suddenly they turned and plodded off into the trees. He exhaled a great sigh of relief. Afterwards he concluded that they must have been Crows.

Two days later, he crossed a large valley, and now the land was rimmed by blue, snow-patched ridges. That afternoon, genuine signs of civilization appeared for the first time. Snow was falling heavily as he approached a farmhouse and knocked on the door. After a cautious welcome, he was given a good square meal beside a warm fire and he realized he was among decent folks. They were Norwegian immigrants. He stayed for three days, embarrassed by the fact that he had no money to give them, but they said that they were Christians and wanted no payment for helping a stranger in need. Instead, he chopped a huge stack of kindling for them. He also saw the interest the man and his son showed in his pony and he tried to give it to them, but they insisted on paying him, and as well as cash they gave him a warm coat and a hat. Then he set out to cover the remaining miles on foot. The pony had served him well, but the travelling had left the beast's unshod hoofs worn, and it needed shoeing and time to recover. He did not begrudge anything to the immigrants.

Snow was falling and an icy wind drove into him as he plodded along.

When he eventually reached Virginia City, the civilization he found was of the harsh variety. On the outskirts, a body was dangling from a tree, the neck twisted at an unnatural angle, the mouth open in a vain attempt to avoid choking to death. Pinned to the trunk of the tree was a card upon which were scrawled the words: *This ruffian was hanged by the Vigilance Committee after a fair trial for killing Fred Maple. He dangles here as a warning to others who may consider disturbing the peace.*

Signed: Elias Prettyman, Captain of Vigilance Committee.

Jared walked on, taking consolation in that it was most unlikely word of his misdemeanours had preceded him. He figured the army was too busy with the Indians to spread word about him, and even so, it was not a civil offence that he had committed.

But he was overlooking the hatred harboured by certain individuals.

Virginia City was a new-founded settlement, which had grown up quickly as gold was discovered in the nearby gulches. The lust for quick wealth drew men like flies to a carcass. Most of its population had made the long tortuous journey through Idaho, the Bozeman Trail still too dangerous from the Indian threat. The majority of the buildings were low shacks and stores. A few taller buildings were merely false-fronts. Already the inevitable appetites of men were being pandered to, with saloons and bawdy-houses. It seemed strange to Jared to have people bustling around him again, though none showed any interest in him. Many had oriental faces. He pondered on what he should now do. Civilization was all very well, but he needed money.

That afternoon the snow eased off and the sun shone. Walking through the slush at the end of Wallace Street, he noticed a crowd of men gathered around a poster. He joined the throng and read what it said.

IRISH JACK IS PLEASED TO ANNOUNCE THAT ANY MAN WHO CAN REMAIN ON HIS FEET FOR TEN MINUTES IN A FAIR FIGHT (LONDON PRIZE-RING RULES), WILL BE AWARDED A PRIZE OF 50 DOLLARS. KICKING, GOUGING, HEAD-BUTTING, BITING AND LOW HITTING WILL ONLY BE TOLERATED IN EXTREME CIRCUMSTANCES. ADMISSION IS FREE TO ALL THOSE ACCEPTING THIS CHALLENGE, IRISH JACK WILL START TAKING ON CHALLENGERS AT 7.30 THIS EVENING.

Jared recalled how he had outfoxed Horse Millard, despite the sergeant's knuckleduster. Now, he could certainly do with fifty dollars. He decided to take up the challenge, so he rested during the afternoon at the Bale of Hay saloon and listened to a man playing a piano organ. At the appointed time he reported to the little box-office that had been set up and said he would like to challenge Irish Jack. He was given a free entrance-ticket into a big tent which had a ring, some twenty-feet square, roped off as an arena. The place was lit by oil lamps, suspended from the roof, and these swayed in the draught, casting dancing shadows of the tent-poles across the assembly. Business was good. Side-bets were being taken and already the wooden benches were occupied by a rowdy gathering. The sight of the giant bare-chested man who was posturing on a platform, exchanging banter with the crowd, was far from reassuring. Irish Jack had huge biceps and fists, and he looked a good six-and-a-half feet tall.

'He's almost as big as Elias Prettyman!' somebody yelled, and this brought a ripple of nervous laughter.

Jared wondered who Elias Prettyman was, then recalled that he was chairman of the Vigilance Committee, and that there was a body hanging by the neck to prove his authority.

Three other challengers were waiting at the side of the platform, but one of these, having gazed at Irish Jack for a moment, departed, his face decidedly pale. Jared considered following him, but before he could do so, a man appeared and listed down the names of the remaining challengers. Jared gave his as Jim Foster, deeming it imprudent to advertise his true identity. Along the wall of the tent, he noticed that a so-called 'professor of medicine' had set up a stall displaying LINIMENT AND MEDICATION SUITABLE FOR BRUISES AND OTHER INJURIES CAUSED BY PRIZE-FIGHTING.

Being last to arrive, Jared had to wait while the other challengers squared up to Irish Jack. He towered over each of them, fighting with bared knuckles amid the hoots and jeers of the crowd. Neither contender lasted for more than a couple of minutes, being carried bleary-eyed and battered from the ring. Jared concluded that they could both have fought Irish Jack at the same time and it would have made no difference. He wondered uneasily if he would do any better, but now it was too late to turn back.

After a rub down with a towel, Irish Jack called for the next challenger. Jared stripped to the waist, climbed through the ropes and shook the man's paw. Irish Jack seemed in a good humour, for he gave Jared a wry grin as he raised his fists. Jared did likewise, and a second later they were circling around, sizing each other up. *Ten minutes*, Jared thought, *ten minutes to remain on my feet and fifty dollars will be mine*. But even as the thought passed through his brain, Irish Jack sprang forward, and caught him with an open hand across his cheek, bringing cheers from the watchers. It was a sort of warning, a taunt, that could so easily have been a closed fist and cracked his jaw, but it angered Jared. He imagined that it was Horse Millard before him and he lunged in with flailing fists. To his delight he caught his opponent on the chin, making Irish Jack grunt because it was the first blow he had taken that evening. To pass it off, he dropped his fists, inviting Jared to have another try. Jared did not oblige, holding back while the crowd jeered. The big Irishman responded by charging forward, driving Jared almost into the spectators, but he kept his feet and bounced back, ducking beneath his opponent's arm and swung around.

On a table at the side was a big clock, ticking away

the seconds with a slow sweep of its hand. Jared realized he had been fighting for no more than two minutes. It seemed like twenty-four hours, or was the clock intentionally slow? But then he figured Irish Jack would not need a slow clock. Jared was already feeling the strain. His physical strength in no way matched that of Irish Jack, but he was not going to give in. When the Irishman caught him a sharp blow across the side of his jaw, sent him staggering back, he kept his feet and counter-attacked. He was aware of the crowd all around, a blur of faces, shouting – and suddenly he realized that their cheers were for him. This gave him a fresh surge of determination, and to his satisfaction his fist connected with Irish Jack's chin, making the man grunt, but not removing the confident grin that seemed permanently on his face.

For a moment they drew back from each other, circling, Jared fighting for breath against the constricting pressure on his lungs. He risked a quick glance at the clock and was relieved to see that the big hand had crept around and that he had just three minutes to remain standing. It seemed like a lifetime since he had entered the ring and he knew that there was blood running down his cheek.

But suddenly Irish Jack seemed to become aware of the seconds ticking away and he let out an intimidating bellow and came for Jared like a springing panther, incredibly light on his feet for such a large man. Jared was forced back by what seemed a whirlwind of great fists, desperately striving with his forearms to ward off blow after blow, sensing suddenly that he had been foolishly over-confident in taking on this man who knew every trick in his pugilistic trade. He tried to step back out of trouble, and that was when Irish Jack's fist connected with his jaw, and everything was spinning around him and his legs felt like jelly. Another blow hammered into his jaw and suddenly he was on the boards and his consciousness was something he could no longer keep a grip on.

He did not know how much later it was, but he had been propped into a sitting position and his back was being slapped and words of congratulation were filling his ears. It seemed he was drowning in a sea of grinning faces. His head felt as if it was a cracked egg with a chick struggling to break free. He groaned. He reached up and touched his swollen chin. He wondered if it was broken. He flexed his jaw and was thankful that, at least, he could open his mouth. He felt in desperate need of air, tried to stand up, failed, but then was helped by the men around him. He realized that Irish Jack was looming over him, still grinning. Jared had half raised his fists to continue the fight when he realized it was all over.

'You didn't last the ten minutes, young fella,' the Irishman beamed, 'but you sure made a good fight of it. Best challenger I've had in Virginia City.'

This comment was greeted with a wave of cheering and more back-slapping on Jared's weak-kneed body.

When the noise quieted, Irish Jack went on: 'For being such a good sport, I've decided to give you half the prize and wish you better luck next time.'

More cheering and applause thundered as Jared nodded his gratitude, shook the Irishman's great paw, and told himself that there was not going to be a next time, even though he liked Irish Jack. Five minutes later he stepped out into the cool, refreshing night, twenty-five dollars better off.

THIRTEEN

Over the next week, Jared recovered from the bruising he had taken. The boxing-match had gained for him a certain notoriety and he did not welcome this, for the last thing he wanted was anything apart from a low profile. However, his new-found fame brought him several free drinks and a meal at the Bale of Hay saloon, and gave him the time he needed to look around. There was much talk about Elias Prettyman and his vigilantes, mostly in whispered and respectful terms. Virginia City lacked any official law-enforcement, and certain citizens had banded together to keep the peace. During their first year of existence, the vigilantes had lynched twenty-four outlaws, and a good many more since, the crow-picked skeleton hanging on the outskirts of town being a recent example. Elias Prettyman had an awesome reputation and was generally spoken of in hushed and respectful voices.

Gold fever gripped the place like a disease and more men were coming in, greedy to make their fortune. Lots were being sold over the counter of the saloon and Jared decided to try his luck, so he bought himself a lot; it was going cheap because it was said to be worked out. He ensured that it was registered by the barkeeper, and next day walked to Alder Gulch. Here, the river flowed between thick alders which blocked out the sun and kept the place permanently gloomy. Tents and primitive shacks had been erected along the banks and men scurried about like ants. Some waded into the river, panning the shallows, while others toiled waist-deep in the icy water, building a dam to alter the river's course.

More groups slogged with a huge cradle-like contraption. This sat on rockers ten feet long. Working as a team, men spaded sand from the river bed into its trough, poured on water, and rocked the machine until they were exhausted. Other men laboured like grave-diggers, shovelling down to the bed-rock.

Jared found his assigned section on the north side. It was on the fringe of the main activity, at a point where the river twisted into a curve. Soon he had it staked out. Within twenty-four hours he had set himself up with the necessary equipment, having purchased a good pick, a pan, a small tent and other accoutrements on the slate.

Over the next days, he spent hours sluicing the river water with his pan, straining his eyes for glint of gold. This section had not been as played out as was supposed. It was back-breaking work, but on the fourth day he got his first small success and from then on he was as smitten with gold fever as the men around him.

Bitter winter closed in. Plummeting temperatures, ice and snow made life for the prospectors miserable, but work carried on. Around Jared there were an assortment of men – doctors, lawyers, ranchers, carpenters, farmers as well as general riff-raff. You could not tell the difference between them because most were garbed in grey-striped hickory, red-flannel shirts, high boots – with a slouch hat pulled down against the weather. All had one idea – to hit it rich and thereafter live a life of luxury. But fortune never came as fast as men wished and the hardships increased. Men squabbled and flailed their fists. Sickness was rife, mostly scurvy, bad guts and crippling rheumatism because so much time was spent in damp conditions.

Jared had built himself a simple shack way back in the woods – a one-roomed timber frame, covered with branches and earth, with a door he could close to keep out the wind. Somehow he avoided sickness. His constitution had never failed him. He had not panned a fortune by any means, but he had sifted enough gold to make his trips to the assayers in town worthwhile. He was able to pay off his debts, set himself up with warm clothing, a few items of simple furniture, blankets and an adequate supply of provisions. He thus survived the first winter.

One day in early spring he had completed his business at the assayers, checking that the man weighed out his nuggets honestly, and had stepped into the saloon to warm himself by the stove, when he realized that there was a group of soldiers at the far end of the bar. One man, a corporal, turned, just for the briefest moment caught Jared's eye. Jared immediately backed from the place. Once in the street, he ran down a side alley and cut between two warehouse buildings. Over the weeks, he had explored the area and he knew he could throw off any pursuit that might come. As it was, when he did pause for breath and glanced back, there was no evidence that anybody had come after him. Perhaps, even if the corporal remembered him at Fort Phil Kearny, he had not recognized him. After all, his face was now ragged with beard and his hair had grown long. The soldiers must have come up from the fort, perhaps on the look-out for deserters. Their presence had given him an unpleasant shock, reminding him that the past was always there to haunt him.

Later, as he trudged back to his shack through falling snow, he tried to calm his fears. He convinced himself that there was no cause for panic, that the corporal probably had not spared him a second thought. Even so, he determined to be more alert in future.

Sergeant Millard saluted and stood just inside the door of Major Shafter's small office. He had been sent for many times previously, inevitably to be giving a dressing-down. Shafter had ranted and stormed, his face red and twitching, leaving Millard in no doubt that he had let the major down in allowing Private Harris to escape. But today Shafter did not look up. He sat at his desk, hat pulled down as usual, shuffling through reports, until at last Millard coughed to remind him he was here.

At last Shafter deigned to lift his eyes, and then the most unexpected thing happened. He smiled. 'Take a seat, Sergeant. Help yourself to a cigar.'

Millard grunted with surprise, but he was not one to

let a chance pass, especially at this stage in his career.
There was no point in putting his pension in jeopardy,
meagre as it was. Secretly he had agreed for a long
time with what others were saying: that Shafter's
brain was twisted. He sat down, took a cigar from the
box on the desk, bit the end off and accepted a light
from the officer.

'So today is your last day in the service,' Shafter
said, taking a cigar himself.

'Yes, sir. Hand my uniform in tomorrow and pull out
when the wagon train leaves.'

Shafter took a long draw on his cigar and exhaled
smoke towards the ceiling.

'Sergeant, I guess we've had our differences in the
past, mainly over Private Harris.'

'Yes, sir.' Millard felt uneasy. He wondered what all
this was leading up to.

'Well,' Shafter continued, 'maybe we can put things
right. Maybe we can come to an amicable arrange-
ment. As you may know, I come from a wealthy family.
When somebody provides me with a good service, I can
be very generous.'

'I know, sir.' The prospect of money quickened
Millard's interest. 'You want me to do something for
you?'

Shafter nodded. 'A strictly confidential service. Our
conversation must go no further than these walls. I
believe I can trust you.'

'You can, sir.'

'I shall be taking retirement from the army in six
months' time. I shall live at my home in Idaho City. I
will give you the details. If you visit me, one year from

today, with certain news, and certain proof, you'll find yourself richer by fifty thousand dollars.'

Shock had the cigar slipping from Millard's lips. He retrieved it with a juggling act. 'Fifty thousand!' he queried.

'Precisely. You have my word as an officer.'

It took Millard a moment to recover. He had never had such wealth in his life. 'And what, sir, do you want me to do for that money?'

'I want you to track Private Harris down and I want you to kill him without anybody tracing it back to me. Is that clear, Sergeant Millard? Nobody must know, except you and me.'

Millard allowed the proposition to sink into his brain. It was strange. Shafter was offering him fifty thousand dollars to do something he had intended doing anyway.

'And to make the job easier for you,' Shafter said, 'I'll advance you enough money to meet your immediate expenses. Also, I can tell you that Corporal Elkins, when he was with a patrol up at Virginia City, swore blind he spotted Harris and went after him, but lost him in the alleys. It may have been him or it may not, but at least it'll give you somewhere to start looking. Will you take the job on?'

Millard forced himself to look dubious, making the major wait for his reply. Inwardly he felt excited. The fact was, he yearned to see Harris in his grave as much as Shafter; had done ever since the Johnny Reb had eyed up his wife Jessie, and even more so after he had knocked him out cold in the fight. No man had ever done that before. Surviving, after he had been sent to dismantle those tents and what appeared to be certain death, had put the final nail in the Southerner's coffin, as far as Millard was concerned, though he was not going to admit it now.

After a moment he gave his head a nod. 'I'll come to Idaho City in a year's time,' he said. 'I'll bring you the news you want.'

A look of relief swept over Shafter's face. 'Hopefully,' he said, 'we'll both have something to celebrate.' He reached for a whiskey bottle on his shelf. 'Now, let's drink to a successful mission.'

FOURTEEN

The pickings by no means matched the optimism that prevailed in Virginia City and Jared gradually realized that more money was made by those who earned their living by supplying the needs of the prospectors than the prospectors themselves. However everybody seemed convinced that El Dorado lay just around the corner, and every time news came of a lucky strike, fresh enthusiasm surged through him.

He had just collected his supplies at Murphy's Store and was stepping out on to the boardwalk when he got an unpleasant shock. He came face to face with two soldiers he remembered from Fort Phil Kearny. The taller man's name was Fitzsimmons and his eyes were very dark, set back deep in their sockets, somehow depriving his features of mobility. His teeth were heavily stained with baccy. The other man was a short, insignificant individual with shifty eyes and a consumptive cough, and Harris could not recall his name. Both were clad in scruffy civilian clothing, apart from military boots, and there was something in the furtive manner of their movements that told Harris that they had, like him, deserted.

'Well I'll be damned,' Fitzsimmons muttered, 'if it ain't our old pal Johnny Reb Harris. Glad to see the army ain't caught up with you yet.'

Harris nodded. He noticed that both men carried Springfields, no doubt stolen from the army. This was the sort of company he could do without.

'The army doesn't come up here too often,' he said, and then he asked, 'You done a runner too?'

'Sure we have,' Fitzsimmons responded. 'Couldn't stand army rations no longer. Didn't join the army to be treated like dirt. Anyway, we heard the gold pickin's was good up here.'

The other man was nodding in agreement. 'Say,' he said, 'you struck lucky?'

'Nothing much,' Harris said.

Fitzsimmons grinned, displaying his stained teeth. 'If you had, you wouldn't tell us, eh? Where you hangin' out? Found yourself some pretty-lookin' woman?'

Harris wanted to get rid of these men as soon as possible, but they showed signs of sticking around.

The smaller man indulged in a bout of coughing, then said, 'We could sure do with somewhere to hole up for a while. A little hospitality from an old pal. Maybe somethin' to eat.'

'I've got a shack way out of town,' Harris said. 'It's not convenient for visitors. But I'll buy you a drink and a bite to eat over at the saloon, if you like.'

'That would be mighty friendly,' Fitzsimmons nodded.

So Harris led the way over to the saloon and set his

companions up with beer and sandwiches. Once they were seated at a table, he questioned them about life at Fort Phil Kearny. Apparently Sergeant Millard had taken his discharge and had left, along with his woman. He had talked about going prospecting.

'Where?' Harris inquired.

'Didn't say,' Fitzsimmons said. 'I'd watch out if he shows up here. He was right mad at the way you shacked up with his wife and then got away at the Wagon Box camp. Major Shafter gave him a right kick up the ass.'

Jared was angry at the way facts got distorted. He wished he had never set eyes on the woman. She had brought him nothing but trouble. Even now his companions were sniggering at him.

'Shafter,' he said. 'Is he still there?'

Fitzsimmons picked a string of meat from his teeth with long black fingernails. 'Could use another beer,' he said.

Jared obliged both men with more beer, then repeated his question. 'Shafter?'

'Sure he's still there, at least physically. But his brain's off with the fairies, I guess. He stomps around with his hat pulled right low to hide that scar, and his face is fixed in a permanent scowl. He keeps twitchin' and mutterin' to hisself. Can't understand why the army keeps him on in that state. He's real mean with his men, treats everybody like scum. That's why we got out.'

Jared finished his own beer and asked, 'You fellas intend to move on?'

Fitzsimmons exchanged glances with his companion, then said, 'Guess we'll stick around here for a while. Like we said, we could sure do with somewhere to hole up for a week or so. Wouldn't be no trouble.'

Jared stood up. 'Sorry I can't oblige. I'd move on if I was you.'

Fitzsimmons shook his head. 'Zeke and I like it here. We figure we might do a bit of prospectin'. We can do with a lucky strike. Maybe one like you got.'

Harris said, 'I told you. I've not had much.' He knew they didn't believe him. Now, more than ever, he wanted to get away from them. 'Anyway, I wish you luck.'

Fitzsimmons grinned again. 'We'll probably see you around.' He raised his hand in a mock salute and Jared left them sniggering into one of the peep-show machines.

He wondered if they would attempt to follow him. When he reached the outskirts of town, he paused and gazed back along the street. There was plenty of movement back there, but as far as he could ascertain none came from the two deserters. When he reached his hideaway, he pondered on his position. Maybe it was time he moved on, although he had little idea of where he could head. The thought of returning to Kentucky and a home that was a burned-out ruin, a home that no longer had the sparkle of a loving wife, was abhorrent to him. He grieved for Annie and knew he would do until the day he died. There seemed little purpose in a life without her.

He was chopping kindling out front of his shack when he heard somebody approaching through the trees. He paused, tenseness running through him. He was on his feet, when Fitzsimmons and Zeke appeared. Fitzsimmons was grinning. 'Figured we'd pay you a visit, after all,' he said. 'Wasn't hard to follow you out here. Maybe we can stop a night or so.'

'Yeah,' Zeke remarked, then coughed. 'We can talk over old times.'

Harris cursed his stupidity. He should have guessed they would try this. He should have laid a false trail. He was aware that dusk was slipping in. He shrugged his shoulders. Now, there was nothing he could do but humour them.

'Well ... you'd better make yourselves at home. Maybe you can get a fire going. I'll rustle up some grub.'

'That's right friendly,' Fitzsimmons said.

Jared did not trust his visitors. He recalled that Fitzsimmons had had a company record as long as his arm, mostly for drunkenness and unruly behaviour. He did not know much about the other man, Zeke, but he seemed to be in Fitzsimmons's pocket and his eyes darted everywhere inside the shack. He looked sick. Every cough seemed to churn his innards around. They lolled about in the shack, making no effort to assist him in getting the fire going. They watched him as he prepared the food and boiled coffee.

After they had eaten, Fitzsimmons started on about prospecting. 'I reckon we could maybe go into partnership with you.'

Jared shook his head. 'Pickings are not good enough.'

'That's not what I heard,' Zeke cut in. 'One fella told me you could drag nuggets out with the grass roots.'

Jared laughed dismissively and was glad he had a revolver tucked into his waistband. He knew that only a lucky few had made a fortune here at Alder Gulch, and certainly not himself, but at least he had scraped a living over these past months and he was not going to let on to these two that he had a wad of money hidden under his bunk. He tried to turn the conversation to other matters. They gave him the surprising news that the government had been negotiating with the Sioux and it was likely that Fort Phil Kearny would be abandoned.

'It's downright disgraceful,' Zeke said, 'after the way we sweated our guts out buildin' the place. Once it's abandoned, Red Cloud'll burn it down for sure.'

Presently Fitzsimmons wanted to know the best place for women in town and Zeke was nodding vigorously.

Jared told them there was no lack of bawdy-houses.

'Ain't had a woman for six months,' Fitzsimmons said, wiping the grease from his lips with his hand. 'Last woman I had was Jessie Millard, and she was quite something. Only trouble was, she was scared her ol' man would show up and beat hell out o' her. I guess he found out somethin' 'cos she didn't appear for a week, and when she did her face was all bruised and swollen, and I guess the rest o' her sweet body was too.'

Zeke coughed and said, 'That'll teach her for doin' the dirty on her ol' man, eh?'

'She came from a wealthy family, didn't she?' Jared said.

Fitzsimmons laughed scornfully. 'Sure she did. A wealthy bunch of whores in a Bowery flophouse. She never did know who her folks was, but she's a great one for inventin' stories, even though she forgets them the next day.'

'She's got a brain like a randy flea,' Zeke said. 'Say, Harris, everybody reckoned you got up her skirt a few times.'

Jared said nothing, but it sickened him the way false rumours spread.

He did not sleep much that night, making certain his pistol was close at hand and charged ready for action, though Fitzsimmons snored continuously and Zeke coughed monotonously. The visitors arose next morning, treating the place as though they were here to stay.

'Where do you keep all the cash you've made?' Zeke inquired.

Jared did not answer, just shook his head. Presently the two commandeered one of his sifting pans, went down to the river and started panning the water. Meanwhile Jared tried to work out how he could get rid of them. It was not going to be easy, unless he gunned them down and he was not prepared to do that, although he had little doubt that they would not hesitate to shoot him if the fancy took them.

FIFTEEN

Horse Millard and Jessie reached Virginia City the following Sunday, coming in on a wagon train full of prospectors. When they passed the skeleton dangling on the end of a rope, Jessie shuddered and read the inscription beneath the forlorn bones. *This ruffian was hanged by the Vigilance Committee for killing Fred Maple. He dangles here as a warning to others who may consider disturbing the peace.*

Millard booked a room at a boarding-house in Wallace Street. Jessie had dreaded coming to Virginia City until her husband mentioned that Harris might be here. But Millard had figured he saw a glint in his wife's eye and he had cursed and told her that if she took one step out of line, he would strangle her. She seemed to take his words to heart, especially when he mentioned that Shafter was going to give him fifty thousand dollars to kill the Southerner.

'Jessie,' he said in a softer tone, 'you'll get all the pretty dresses and hats you want and maybe some smart jewellery too. You can act like a lady. Just think o' that.' He reckoned the prospect of that sort of money would keep her from misbehaving, no matter how much she thought she fancied Harris.

But the truth was that he had no proof Harris was still in the vicinity of Virginia City, even if he ever had been. Corporal Elkins could very easily have been mistaken. Over the next days, Millard became a regular in all the local saloons and bawdy-houses, striking up drinking-pals and chatting up whores wherever he went, testing them out for news of the man he hunted. But by the end of the second week he had gleaned nothing and he began to consider more desperate action. One thing was certain: he was determined to make that appointment in Idaho City.

Fitzsimmons spotted Jessie Millard on one of the rare occasions she left the boarding-house to go to a nearby store. He had come to town, planning on visiting a whorehouse. She was wearing a dark coat and lace-up boots. He could hardly believe his eyes, but his pulse quickened as he recalled the way he had once taken her behind the stables at Fort Phil Kearny. Right now, she was wrapped in a heavy coat, but he knew that beneath it, her body was rounded and could easily be aroused. He glanced about to make sure her husband was not trailing on, then he followed her into the store and tapped her on the shoulder. She turned nervously, her eyes wide, but when he smiled she relaxed and spoke his name.

'Fitzy!'

'What you doin' here, Jessie? You left your ol' man?'

She shook her head. 'No. He's back at the boarding-house, sleeping off the booze.'

Fitzsimmons looked her up and down. Those big eyes of hers did something to him, gave him a tingling in his loins. 'Jessie Millard . . . still as pretty as a picture. Remember that time behind the stable? You enjoyed that well enough, eh? You deserve a better man than him. You still figure on leavin' him?'

'No,' she said. She glanced around apprehensively. 'If somebody tells him I've been talking to you, or any other man, he'll treat me real bad. I must get back.'

'Why don't you leave him, come with me, Jessie girl? I've got a place outside of town.' He knew that she would most likely be a liability to him, but he figured he could get rid of her whenever he chose. And the mere sight of her had him hankering to run his hands under her dress.

'No, Fitzy,' she said. 'I'm a married woman and . . .'

'If I told you that a certain somebody is sharin' our shack, back there in the woods, it would make a difference.'

'Who?'

'Your fancy man. Jared Harris.'

'Oh . . .' Her big eyes lit up.

He grunted with satisfaction, seeing how her attitude changed. 'I'll come with you, Fitzy,' she whispered, 'but first I need to get a few things from our room. I won't be more than ten minutes.'

He frowned. 'But surely Horse will realize somethin's up?'

She shook her head. 'No. He'll still be asleep. You wait here. I'll be back real quick. Honest, Fitzy,' and she gripped his hand in a reassuring squeeze.

'All right,' he said, 'but be quick.'

She left him, hurried down the street to the boarding-house. She found her bleary-eyed husband sitting up on the bed.

'Horse,' she gasped, 'you'll never guess what. I met Private Fitzsimmons. You remember, he deserted a while back. He wants me to run off with him.'

Millard unleashed an angry snarl.

'Listen,' she went on. 'He says he'll take me to his shack out of town. He says Jared Harris is there.'

'Harris!' Millard snapped to full alertness.

'Yes, if you follow us, keep out o' sight, you'll find him and you can do what has to be done.'

He was on his feet now, strapping on his gun.

When she returned to Fitzsimmons at the store, she was carrying her small valise, excitement radiating from her eyes.

He said, 'Why you been so long? Thought you was never comin' back.'

'I was as quick as I could be. Had to be careful not to wake him up.' She hugged on to his arm, pressing her body against his. 'I wouldn't let you down, Fitzy.'

'OK,' he grunted, 'let's get movin'.'

Together, they stepped out on to the boardwalk. Fitzsimmons grunted with annoyance as he glimpsed a flurry of blue at the end of the street. Jessie followed his gaze and saw that an army patrol, maybe a dozen men, had pulled into town, were dismounting.

'I hear they're offering good money for the capture of deserters,' she said.

Fitzsimmons did not answer but hastened her through the back alleys until they left town and were striking out along the bleak and currently deserted trail that ran through the forest towards Alder Gulch. He tried to strike a fast pace, but she stumbled and slipped in the mud. He turned and dragged her roughly up. She wondered if her husband was following, but she dared not look back in case Fitzsimmons became suspicious. She slowed the pace as much as possible, hoping it would give Horse a better chance. She tried to focus her attention on the fifty thousand dollars that Horse had been promised. Maybe they would go back to New York, somewhere other than the Bowery, and live a life of luxury. Maybe Horse would change, be kind to her. When they had first met, he had made plenty of promises.

Shortly, rain began to fall and the light was fading beneath the towering trees. She hoped Horse would be able to find their trail all right, that last night's drinking had not dulled his senses.

They were both soaked with rain. Fitzsimmons drew up. 'There's a cave up ahead, over on the right,' he gasped, his lips close to her ear, 'maybe we'd better hole up for a while. It'll be real cosy in there.'

She nodded.

Soon, he led her off the trail and through the opening of a gash in the rock. Once in the shadowy interior, they were out of the wind and rain. She heard his throaty laugh. She knew very well what he wanted.

'Come here, Jessie,' he grunted, drawing her against hint, fumbling with the buttons of her coat.

'Not here, Fitzy,' she protested.

He was breathing heavily and even in the dim light she could see the excitement on his face.

'Don't play hard to get,' he whispered hoarsely. 'You

liked it well enough before. Remember . . .'

She laughed nervously. 'Fitzy, that was different. It's so uncomfortable here. It's . . .'

Her protestations gave way as he tore open her coat, his cruel hands hoisting her skirt as his mouth smothered hers. He pressed her against the dank wall of the cave, ripping at her drawers. He was rampant and she knew that she could no longer ward him off, but she was no stranger to men nor the way to satisfy them and she finally gave herself with an abandon that matched his.

They were writhing on the cave floor when what little light there was became blotted out. Millard loomed in the cave entrance. She saw him first. She was sprawled back, moaning, her skirt in disarray. Fitzsimmons was sated and panting, lying heavily across her. The sudden tension in her made him twist. He grunted with shock as he recognized the intruder.

Millard was growling, his bulky frame blocking the entrance like a bear's, his fury like a tangible thing flooding the cave. Suddenly flame stabbed and the blast of his gun bludgeoned Jessie's ears.

But Fitzsimmons had anticipated well, instinct had him rolling to the side, scrambling on the rocky floor as the bullet ricocheted about his head, buzzing like a lethal hornet. He forced himself to his feet, backing against the back wall, realizing he was helpless and could retreat no further.

All at once, Jessie was screaming, 'No . . . don't kill him. Remember Harris. He can lead us to him!'

Millard had drawn the hammer back on his revolver, had it raised for his second shot, but the girl's words pierced through his anger.

'Sure I'll take you to him,' Fitzsimmons cried out, 'if that's what you want.'

Millard hesitated. All three were breathing heavily, poised for what would happen next. At last Millard appeared to relent. 'All right,' he gasped. 'But don't try any tricks. If you do, there'll be a bullet in your dawgone head, Fitzsimmons. I promise that.'

'I'll do whatever you want,' Fitzsimmons murmured in a submissive voice.

Jessie too had scrambled up, smoothing her torn dress and drawing her coat around her. She was trembling violently.

Millard gestured with his gun to Fitzsimmons. 'You come out first, with your hands raised.' He stood back to allow the other man to pass him.

Fitzsimmons reached down, gathered up his hat and put it on.

Jessie watched him as he complied with her husband's order. 'I couldn't help it, Horse,' she sobbed. 'He forced me to . . .' She lowered her eyes to refasten the belt of her coat . . . and that was when the shot blasted off and into its echo a man's scream of agony sounded.

SIXTEEN

Zeke was bubbling over with excitement, so much that it brought on a bout of coughing. He had found a glistening nugget in the mud he had been sifting. He rushed back to the shack, jubilant. Jared had been cleaning things up. Within the small confines of the abode, the last thing he needed was the laziness of his two lodgers. He was glad Fitzsimmons had gone into Virginia City. At least he was out of the way for a few hours.

He allowed Zeke to ramble on about his find. 'How much'll it be worth?' he wheezed.

Jared did not answer.

They both heard somebody approaching through the trees. This was earlier than he had expected Fitzsimmons to return. Jared picked up his gun, checked it and tucked it in his waistband ready for action. But nothing could prepare him for the sight of Jessie Millard stumbling into the clearing. Behind her came Fitzsimmons looking downright angry.

'Jared!' Jessie cried, and she ran forward and threw herself into his arms. 'Thank God you're here.'

He was quite taken aback by her outburst, but he tried to calm her down.

'I met her in town,' Fitzsimmons was explaining. 'She begged me to help her escape from her ol' man.'

'Was Millard in town as well?' Jared asked, feeling uneasy at the man's possible proximity.

'He *was*,' Fitzsimmons responded evasively.

But Jessle was gushing on. 'He followed us out of town and Fitzy shot him . . . dead! He lulled Horse into thinking he was beaten, but he had a gun in his boot-top.'

'My God!' Jared gasped. 'Horse Millard . . . dead!'

Fitzsimmons glanced at Zeke. 'Come on,' he said. 'We're gettin' out o' here.'

'But, Fitzy. Just when the pickin's are good,' Zeke argued. 'We—'

'I told you,' Fitzsimmons shouted. 'We're gettin' out! They got this crazy idea of lynching fellas out o' hand here. Ain't no fair trial or nothin'. I ain't stickin' around to get strung up for killin' a rat like Millard.'

'You taking Jessie with you?' Jared demanded.

Fitzsimmons shook his head. 'She'll be safer with you.' He wasn't wasting time for further talk. He gathered up what few possessions he had from the shack. Zeke did likewise, coughing as he went, never being one to argue with his bigger companion, and within ten minutes they were on their way, hurrying northward through the trees.

Jessie seemed stunned by events, but she turned to Jared and said, 'It was awful. We thought we could get away, had given Horse the slip, but somehow he found out, followed us and tried to kill Fitzy. But Fitzy tricked him. Shot Horse clean in the chest. Even so, he staggered down the slope, screaming out and spilling blood all over the place. Eventually, he dropped down, and when we reached him, he was dead.'

'I guess you're grief-stricken, Jessie,' he said.

She gave him a grin. 'Like hell, I am. Especially now I got you, Jared. There's nothing to keep us apart now.'

'But, Jessie, there's one thing you've got to understand,' he said. 'I don't love you, never did.'

'You will, Jared. I'll give you whatever you want and more. I know how to make a man happy. I'll be your woman, no messing.'

He sighed heavily, then said, 'You better come inside. At least I'll give you something to eat.'

'And somewhere to sleep for the night?' she inquired.

He nodded resignedly and they entered the shack.

As Jessie followed him, he did not see the strange look that appeared on her face. She told herself that Jared Harris was no better than any other man, though once she had thought he was. Her thoughts dwelt on the fifty thousand dollars that James Shafter had promised for the killing of this man. Horse could not complete the mission now, but she could, and she had no doubt that the major would be equally generous to her, if she could provide evidence of the Southerner's death. She regretted that she had no gun. She eyed the pistol tucked in Jared's waistband. She would use her charms to acquire it. She would lull him into trusting her, then . . .

'Jessie,' he said as he breathed life into his fire, 'how come you and Horse came to Virginia City?'

'He came looking for you. You see Major Shafter offered him fifty thousand dollars if he'd kill you.'

'Fifty thousand dollars!' Jared whistled his surprise. He could not understand it. 'Why was Shafter so anxious to see me dead? Was it because I escaped from the Wagon Box camp?'

She shook her head. 'I don't know, Jared, but he sure wants you dead.' Then, seeing she had his attention and his apparent trust, she went on. 'Horse was to kill you and then go to Shafter's home in Idaho City to collect the money. It was a crazy, wicked idea. I pleaded with him not to do it, but he wouldn't listen. I came with Horse because I felt I had to stop him killing you.'

He gave her an odd look. 'Not because you wanted your share of the money?'

A look of horror spread across her face. 'No Jared. You know I love you, always did since I first set eyes on you back at the fort. I hated the way Horse treated you, but you never retaliated and that made him even madder.'

He nodded.

'Now he's dead,' she rambled on, 'and he can't do you no more harm, can't stand between us again.'

Later, after they had eaten and it was dark apart from the glimmer of the fire, he spread a blanket for her at the spot Fitzsimmons had used, but she said, 'Let me sleep in your arms, Jared, somewhere I know I'll be safe. I won't ask for anything more than your warmth, not unless you want it. I just want to be naked and with you.'

He hesitated, then nodded. She watched him remove his gun and place it on the far side of his bunk. 'There's not much room, Jessie,' he said.

'I don't need much room,' she murmured.

She undressed, her body showing pale white in the dim light, then she slipped into the bunk beside him. She undid the buttons of his shirt and pressed her breasts against him. For a moment she felt her passions rising, and she whispered his name over and over, but he made no effort to respond and she grew frustrated. No man had ever slept with her and displayed such utter lack of passion. She grew angry. Her pride had been wounded. Very well, if that was the way he wanted it . . .

Her mind turned to her earlier intentions, dwelling on the wealth that awaited in Idaho City. She would not even have to share it with Horse. She could have all the dresses and jewellery and any man she chose. It was incredible how things had worked out. Everything had been handed to her on a plate. There was only one task she needed to complete. She suddenly hated Jared. He had insulted her.

She waited until his breathing steadied, and when she glanced at him in the glimmer of what was left of the fire, he was lying with his eyes firmly shut and his mouth slightly open. She decided it was time to make her move. Very slowly she disentangled herself from his arms, checked to convince herself that he was still asleep, and eased herself out of the bunk. Crawling on her hands and knees on the cold earth floor, she made her way around to where the gun was on the side stool. Her hands closed over its cold metal, she took a deep breath, exhilaration running through her. This was going to be surprisingly easy!

'Jessie,' he said, 'it's no good you getting hold of that

gun. I took the precaution of removing the bullets from it.'

She dropped the gun with a thud on to the floor. 'Jared,' she sobbed angrily, 'I never meant . . .'

'Sure, Jessie,' he said. 'I guess you'd better spend the rest of the night in that blanket over there. I'm not feeling affectionate.'

He did not sleep any more that night. Jessie had pulled on her clothes and taken to the other blanket and she sobbed for a long time until eventually she went quiet and he guessed she was sleeping. But she was not. She was filled with remorse. She could not understand herself. What had come over her? Could she really have killed this man while he slept?

But he was not going to take any chances of her tricking him. She was as unpredictable as a snake. He wished he had taken her when she had wanted him. He could have kept her under control that way, avoided her ire from being roused, and maybe that would have stopped her from doing mad things like looking for his gun. It had been a blessing that she had believed the gun was not loaded.

He kept the fire burning, feeding in wood which caused it to crackle and spit and that was why, as the first glimmer of dawn came, he did not hear the arrival of his visitors until it was too late.

The voice sounded like the wrath of Heaven: 'Come out with your hands raised. We got you surrounded. One false move and we'll riddle you with bullets!'

Jessie was sitting up in her blanket, her big eyes wide with fear. 'Jared . . . who is it!'

He knew who it was all right. Elias Prettyman and

his self-appointed vigilantes.

In those few pulsating seconds, they both heard the rattle of rifles being cocked from outside – an ominous, threatening sound that brought their senses to full sharpness.

'Come out you killers, with your hands raised. We ain't tellin' you again!' The voice had an insane urgency about it.

'They must've found Horse's body,' Jessie sobbed.

'Well, you didn't do the killing,' Jared said, 'and they've got nothing on me.'

At that moment a shot blasted off and the bullet tore into the shack's frail timber, bringing down a shower of earth from the roof, and Jessie was screaming. Jared knew that unless they obeyed, a swath of lead would cut them down. His only hope was to try and talk sense into Prettyman and his crew.

'Come on,' he said to the woman, 'we have no choice.'

She nodded, but he could hear the frightened pant of her breathing, sense the tremble that engulfed her body.

He lifted his hands and stepped out through the shack's doorway into the cold light of dawn. The woman cringed behind him, using his body to shield her if they chose to open fire.

Jared took in the line of riders, seven of them, sitting their horses, all training their guns on him. They were all wearing black hoods. He could see their eyes through the slits. There was no doubt about the giant of a man who sat slightly ahead of the others, despite his hood. Elias Prettyman.

'We're takin' you in,' Prettyman said in the same

loud voice that had at first roused them. 'We're takin' you in for killin' Horse Millard. You and the woman.'

'I never killed Horse!' Jessie shrieked.

'Neither did I,' Jared got out.

This brought a ripple of laughter from the vigilantes.

'You try tellin' that to the Good Lord when you reach them pearly gates,' Prettyman snarled. 'We all know how you ran off with the girl. No wonder her poor husband chased after you. Never dreamed you'd butcher him the way you did.'

Jared did not argue, knowing that it was useless. He had already been judged guilty by these men.

'Tie them up,' Prettyman ordered, and two of his men slid from their horses, uncoiling their ropes.

'What are you goin' to do with us?' Jessie cried in a voice trembling with terror.

'We're goin' to take you back to town,' Prettyman explained. 'You'll get a fair trial and hangin'. We'll leave you strung up as a warning to other folk, men and women, who want to break the law.'

'No . . .' Jessie screamed. 'I never did nothing.'

'Whatever she did,' the man on Prettyman's right said, 'we can't hang no woman, wouldn't be right.'

Prettyman unleashed a scornful laugh. 'Can't we? You'll damn well see!'

With rifles still trained on them, Jared and Jessie were each circled with rope that was knotted tightly, then, like performing bears on chains, they were forced to walk.

Over those tortuous miles, Jessie fell several times but was dragged up, profanity raining down about her.

The new day took hold. Jared plodded along, his mind searching frantically for some means of escape. He knew that these men were totally unreasonable, that they were convinced that it was him who had left town with Jessie, convinced that he and the woman had contrived to murder her indignant husband. Jared knew that they would be placed before some mockery of a court, and that Prettyman would have no compunction at stringing them up alongside the other man, whose bones still remained suspended, picked clean by the birds, bleached by the sun. Jared figured he had only one slim chance, and that was if the person who had originally seen Jessie leave town with a man, would swear that it was not him. But he knew he was clutching at straws. Elias Prettyman and his vigilantes created such fear in the community that nobody would cross them in their deadly work, at least not to save a stranger who had always kept to himself – just one of the hundreds who had come to purge the land of gold.

By the time they reached town, Jessie was exhausted. She had kept sobbing throughout her stumbling journey, becoming hysterical, but this brought her no compassion from the self-righteous bullies who forced them on. Jared maintained his grim silence, inwardly praying that some means of hope would appear before it was too late. One thing was certain. Every second that passed brought them that much closer to the lynch rope.

True enough, their so called 'fair trial' proved to be an absolute farce. They were taken to a barnlike building on the outskirts of town, and, still bound, were made to stand before the same vigilantes who had brought them in. There were no other witnesses. Prettyman demanded their names and jotted some notes on a scrap of paper, then read aloud the charge of murdering Horse Millard. He then asked if there was anything they wished to say.

Jessie somehow steadied herself. In desperation she blurted out that it was not she who had done the killing. That she was just a poor simple woman who had been taken advantage of. She had not ever dreamed of murdering her dear, loving husband, so she pleaded.

Her gabbled words must have struck a chord because the vigilantes listened her out, then Prettyman asked, 'Well, if what you say is true, will you confirm that this man, Jared Harris, did the killing?'

'If I tell you the truth,' Jessie sobbed out, 'will you let me go?'

One of the other vigilantes called out, 'I always said we shouldn't hang no woman. That ain't justice.'

Prettyman hushed him with a wave of his gloved hand. 'You speak the truth, Jessie Millard, and we'll consider what's to be done with you.' And then in a louder voice he demanded, 'It *was* Harris who killed your husband, wasn't it?'

Jared waited for Jessie's next words, holding his breath. Prettyman's question seemed to hang in the air. He repeated it, his voice ugly with impatience. *'It was Harris who murdered your husband. Speak now or you'll go to the rope with him.'*

Jessie seemed to wilt. She nodded her head. 'Yes, yes. It was him.' And she would have fainted away had the vigilante standing alongside her not grabbed her.

Prettyman sighed with satisfaction. 'Cut her loose,' he ordered.

Jared was sickened. He opened his mouth to speak, but in the sudden uproar his words of denial went unheeded.

Only when some order had been restored, did Prettyman's voice come again. 'Jared Harris, you are found guilty of murdering Horse Millard. I therefore sentence you to be hung by the neck until you are dead, so help me God!'

SEVENTEEN

Rough, merciless hands clawed at Jared. He struggled but was cuffed into submission. He was surrounded by angry, frenzied men, their heads shrouded in ugly hoods. It was worse than all his nightmares rolled into one. He was helpless as he was bundled out through the barn entrance amid jeers and dragged down the street.

Somehow word had got round that the vigilantes had caught a murderer. Already people were gathering, jeering and waving their fists at Jared; even floozies from the bawdy-houses were standing on the porch of the Bale of Hay, drawing flimsy gowns about their pale bodies. It seemed that the whole world was baying for his blood, like a giant pack of wolves.

And then through the seething mass of people, Jared got sight of something else, something which he had hoped never to see again. The blue of army uniforms.

A few minutes earlier, the detachment from Fort Phil Kearny had become aware of the commotion at the edge of the town, the gathering of a noisy crowd,

132

and Sergeant Curtis had waved his men away, having no intention of interfering in civil matters.

Suddenly the sergeant glimpsed a flurry of movement on his left and reined back fiercely, but he was unable to prevent his horse running a woman down. She had practically hurled herself into the rutted street, colliding in her frantic haste with the animal's chest, having it whinnying and rearing up and Sergeant Curtis struggling for control. The woman had fallen into the mud, like a fluttering bird.

Curtis struggled to prevent his animal's hoofs from trampling her and eventually restored calm. Meanwhile, Corporal Smith had dismounted and was stooping over the woman. For a second he thought she was dead, but then she stirred and he helped her on to her shaky legs.

'My God,' Corporal Smith uttered, 'it's Sergeant Millard's missus.'

The detachment had now reined in and somebody else said, 'It's her all right.'

Curtis gazed at the woman. She meant nothing to him. He had only been posted in to Fort Phil Kearny recently, but men still spoke of Sergeant Millard with some awe.

'Where's your husband, Mrs Millard?' he inquired.

She gave him a crazed glance. He had seldom seen a woman so terrified-looking. She pointed towards the gathering crowd further down the street. 'They were goin' to hang me, but they let me go 'cos I didn't do it!'

'Do what?' Curtis asked.

'Kill Horse,' she gasped. 'I never did it!'

'Well, they're sure fixin' a lynching down the street,'

Corporal Smith cut in. 'They got the fella who did it, eh?'

'I've got to get away from here,' she sobbed, struggling to be free of the corporal's restraining arm, but he did not let go.

'They got the fella who killed ol' Millard?' he repeated.

'No,' she said, shooting him an exasperated look. 'They got somebody else.'

'Who they got?'

She hesitated. She was frantic to escape from this place. She saw expectant faces all around her, waiting for her answer. She could see they would not let her go until she answered. She gave the only answer she could imagine would direct their attention elsewhere.

'They got an army deserter called Jared Harris, but it wasn't him who killed Horse!'

'Jared Harris!' Corporal Smith exclaimed. At that moment he lost his grip on the squirming woman and she immediately ran off, disappearing between some stores.

'Jared Harris ... who's he?' Sergeant Curtis demanded.

'He deserted at the time of the Wagon Box fight. Major Shafter went crazy about gettin' him back.'

'Shafter went crazy all right,' somebody commented. 'Still damn well is.'

'We better take a look before they hang him,' Curtis said and the detail moved forward at a trot. The very purpose of their mission had been to apprehend deserters, but they had never expected a situation like this.

Meanwhile, Jessie Millard plunged between some

dilapidated shacks, her mind filled with only one desire: to get away from this place, to get away from the awful sin she had conunitted in lying about Jared's guilt. Her body still ached from the bruising it had taken when she had collided with the horse. She felt weak from her ordeal, and suddenly she tripped on a clump of wood and fell. She lay, her breath coming in rasps – and suddenly she felt a presence looming over her, and she lifted her terrified eyes to see a figure clad in black peering down at her, the face completely in shadow. As his hand gripped her shoulder, she screamed.

The military detachment reached the clamouring mob and individuals drew back to avoid being trampled by the horses. A feverish, fiendish excitement prevailed. A hanging was the most exciting event that could happen, next to striking gold.

The rope had already been tossed over a crossbeam at the corner of Wallace and Van Buren Streets. The condemned man was standing with his hands tied behind his back, guarded by several hooded vigilantes.

Jared had resigned himself to death, knowing that he was as helpless to resist it as a drowning man was with waves closing over his head. Everything seemed sharp and hard as he grasped at his last sensations of life before he was lynched to eternity. For a second he believed he saw his wife Annie's smiling face close to his own, her eyes bright with love. Her arms were reaching out for him. A warmth spread through him, shutting out the bedlam that surrounded him.

He did not hear the confirming words of Corporal

Smith. 'Yes, Sarge, that's Harris all right!'

Sergeant Curtis responded immediately, his voice coming strongly above the general noise. 'I demand that this prisoner be handed over to military jurisdiction to face charges of desertion.'

Jared roused himself from his stupor, aware that something untoward was happening.

It was Elias Prettyman who stepped forward, bristling with anger, his barrel-like chest thrust out. 'He's been fairly tried for murder and found guilty,' he proclaimed. 'He's due a hangin' right now.'

This was greeted by a howl of approval from the mob.

'I speak on behalf of General Spedding, the Commanding Officer of the District,' Curtis responded authoritatively. 'I demand that this man is handed over immediately. We'll pay you fifty dollars which is the official rate for deserters apprehended by civil authorities.'

Meanwhile, every man of the military detail had unsheathed his carbine, adopting a threatening stance. The mob was drawing back, fearing that bullets might start flying.

Prettyman flapped his arms in disgust, ripped off his hood to display his angry, rugged features. He cursed long and hard, took a long look at the carbines levelled at him, then turned to one of his men, practically choking on his words.

'Cut the bastard free.'

And so it was, amid a bedlam of booing from the mob, Jared was released from the vigilantes' ropes, and these were replaced by military handcuffs. He was hoisted up behind one of the soldiers and the detachment forced a passage through the frustrated crowd.

Next day, the detail started out on the long and uncomfortable journey down the Bozeman Trail back to Fort Phil Kearny. At night, Jared was unable to sleep. He lay shackled, hardly able to believe that he had fallen into the hands of the army again. His escape from lynching had been but a temporary reprieve. He knew that the most serious charge he faced was sleeping on duty, and this offered little hope beyond death at the hands of a firing squad.

As they progressed, Sergeant Curtis ensured that his men were on constant alert for sign of Indians, but the journey was made without any red molestation. On arrival at Fort Phil Kearny the prisoners were consigned to the guard house. Three other prisoners were also being held. There had been a fourth, but Jared soon learned that he had somehow got hold of a knife, slashed his wrists and bled to death.

EIGHTEEN

The prisoners were informed that in due course they would be conveyed to Fort Laramie where they would face trial. Hardly had Jared had time to settle into the small cell, when he was marched to the blacksmith's where he was fitted with a heavy ball and four-foot chain shackled to rings around his ankle. The shackling process was painful, chafing his legs, but he received no mercy.

'You'll be wearing 'em until sentence is carried out,' the corporal in charge advised, 'so you might as well get used to 'em.'

Over the next days, Jared withdrew into himself, complying with orders and having no stomach to converse with the others. He wondered if Major Shafter was still at the post, but was informed by one of the guards that the major had become ill and had left Phil Kearny. Rumours buzzed around their heads. There was talk amongst the guards about the new treaty that had been drawn up with the Indians, that the fort was to be abandoned and this confirmed what he had heard from Fitzsimmons. It grieved him to

138

think that Fitzsimmons and Zeke had escaped capture, but he soon realized that he had too many concerns on his own hands to worry about them.

As arranged, the prisoners, still shackled, were conveyed in wagons along the three-hundred-mile trail to Fort Laramie. It was now June and the days and nights were torrid, mosquitoes and flies a constant pest. He recalled how John 'Portugee' Phillips had covered this same trail through a raging blizzard and he marvelled at the man's fortitude. As for himself, all he could do was curse the ball that he had to drag around.

A week later they were at Fort Laramie. The fort was spread over a large meadow, a much more solid structure than Phil Kearny, having been long established, but his chance of viewing it was soon limited to the four walls of the guardhouse basement cell. This place was even harsher than the cells at Phil Kearny. It was a large room with a rough, whitewashed-stone floor. Here, there were some ten prisoners already confined. There was only one heavily barred door and the smallest of windows for ventilation. There was no furniture and little light. Each man was given a blanket. Within this barren room, they were to eat, sleep and perform their bodily functions in a single, overflowing tub. When their meagre rations were served that evening, the guard sergeant stated that the court martial of Private Jared Harris was scheduled for the following week.

To Jared, the next days slipped by like sand running through an egg-timer. He had the feeling that he was on a icy slope, helpless to avoid sliding into the black, gaping hole at its end. Most of the prisoners did little else but lapse into moroseness and profanity. They were trapped in a cesspit of clanging chains, sliding locks and sharp-spoken orders, and the generally held opinion was that the courts martial would prove just a formality, that a judgment of guilty had already been made.

Just two days before the scheduled trial, an officer arrived and took a statement from Jared.

The court martial was convened at the appointed time in the long, narrow room that was the adjutant's office. The officers on the board wore full dress-uniforms, complete with plumed hats, sashes and epaulettes, and a clerk sat to one side ready to make notes. Colonel Hardcastle acted as judge-advocate. He was a rotund officer with a large mutton-chop moustache and bushy sideburns. He had lost his left arm in the war and his empty sleeve was neatly pinned up. He retained a grim expression, gazing over the top of his gold-rimmed spectacles to meet Jared's eye in intimidating scrutiny. It was as if he was even now reaching a decision as to whether the accused should live or die. Jared, who had been issued with a uniform, had little doubt that this man could sway the board of officers to reach whatever verdict he judged fit. He doubted that he would show compassion towards anyone who had fought for the Confederacy.

Jared was not represented by any formally appointed counsel, his interests supposedly protected by the judge-advocate who also acted as prosecutor for the United States Army.

After the board had been sworn in, Jared was charged with two offences under the Articles of War, those of desertion and sleeping while on duty. When asked to enter a plea, he remained silent as per previous instructions, was thus judged to have pleaded 'not guilty' and the trial commenced.

He knew that his only chance of avoiding the most severe punishment was to relate his entire experiences. When, at last, he gave his statement, his voice came firmly. He explained what had happened at Shiloh. He followed this with claims that he had been victimized by Sergeant Millard who appeared to dislike him because he was a Southerner and a former officer, and that Millard had accused him of molesting his wife. This he adamantly denied. He further explained how, in his own belief, he had been drugged at the Wagon Box camp and this caused him to sleep on guard duty, which was something he had never done before. Afterwards, Millard had ordered him to dismantle the tents in the face of enemy fire, a duty that seemed tantamount to a death sentence. And finally, facing such dire consequences, he had had little option but to escape when he had the chance.

At this point, one of the majors on the board addressed him.

'Major Shafter should have been here today to give evidence, but sadly he is too sick to attend. He has sent in a written report.' He held up a paper. 'Private Harris, were you aware that Major Shafter was at Shiloh and received grievous wounds?'

'I heard that, yes sir,' Jared responded.

'But you did not come into personal combat with him?'

'Not to my knowledge.'

'You did not kick him while he was on the ground?'

'Definitely not, sir. I would not do such a thing.'

At this point the questioning major coughed as if to emphasize the fact that he believed he was hearing lies. 'Your word against the word of a regular officer,' he said and sat down.

More questions followed which Jared answered to the best of his ability. None seemed to add much relevance to either defence or prosecution and eventually he was ordered to stand down.

At this moment an orderly entered the room and whispered something to the judge-advocate. The latter nodded and announced that there was another witness.

'Call Mrs Jessie Millard.'

Jared straightened in astonishment as a pale and trembling Jessie Millard was ushered into the room. She was wearing a modest dress of dark blue, high at the neck. She was accompanied by a man in a dark clerical suit, obviously a reverend. He remained at the back of the room while Jessie was escorted forward. She paused and her big eyes met Jared's in a long unsmiling stare, then she was nudged forward by the orderly. She was asked to confirm her identity and after this she was sworn in, her hand on a Bible, her voice coming so softly and hesitatingly that the judge-advocate asked her to speak up. Somehow she managed this, but she was swaying on her feet as if she was about to faint. She was offered a chair and she sat down.

The board asked her to confirm details about her presence at Fort Phil Kearny and the fact that she had been Sergeant Millard's wife and she responded in the affirmative.

'Why have you come here today, Mrs Millard?'

She glanced nervously to the back of the room and received a reassuring nod from the reverend.

'I came because I have been wicked,' she said, her voice somehow firming up. 'I came because in Virginia City my soul was saved by the Reverend William Elliot. He found me when I was lost. He took me in and cared for me.'

'I see. But why are you here today?'

She cleared her throat. 'I confessed my sins – everything. I told Reverend Elliot about Jared Harris, and how I had lied about him murdering my husband, and how he never did no such thing and how it was Fitzy Fitzsimmons that did it. Reverend Elliot prayed for me to God, and he told me that I must come to this court and tell everything I knew.'

'I see.'

The judge-advocate took over the questioning. 'Mrs Millard, were you aware that your husband victimized any of the men in his charge?'

She hesitated, then nodded. 'Yes, sir. This man, Jared Harris. Horse made his life a misery because he hated Southerners, and Jared Harris was cleverer than him and had been an officer. He was jealous.'

'Would your husband have killed Harris if he could have?'

'Yes. He tried to get him killed at the Wagon Box camp, but he escaped. My husband was furious. And so was Major Shafter.'

'Did Major Shafter dislike Harris?'

'Yes, sir. Even worse than Horse.'

'Why?'

'I don't know. It was something that happened in the war, I think.'

'Mrs Millard, did you ever have an affair with Private Harris?'

'No, sir. We never did nothing.'

There was a pause, then Major Hardcastle asked: 'Did you hear that Harris had been drugged into going to sleep while on guard?'

Jessie looked around, her eyes wide with nervousness. The judge-advocate repeated the question, and she seemed to wilt under the pressure, great shudders going through her body.

'N-no,' she sobbed. 'I never heard about that. B-but Horse told me how the Major wanted Jared Harris d-dead.'

It all suddenly seemed too much for her. She plunged her face into her hands and burst into tears. One of the majors on the board sprang forward and gave her a handkerchief. The judge-advocate told her to stand down. The reverend came from the back of the room and put a supporting arm around her. Jared heard him murmur: 'You have done well, my dear.'

After a brief discussion between the judge-advocate and the other officers, the court was adjourned. The findings would be announced on the next morning.

As Jared was led back to the guardhouse, he passed Jessie and whispered his thanks, knowing that coming here had been a great ordeal for her. But she did not respond. She seemed in a trance. He glanced at the pointed features of the Reverend Elliot and exchanged a nod with him.

When the board was alone, the judge-advocate presided over the findings.

Colonel Hardcastle had more than a casual interest in the case of Private Harris. He was a friend of Colonel Carrington, whom, in his opinion, had been replaced as commanding officer at Fort Phil Kearny quite unjustly. The full disgrace of the Fetterman débâcle had been heaped on his shoulders, and from the ashes of this grim affair, Major James Shafter had been acclaimed a hero for his achievement in repelling the Indians in the Wagon Box Fight. The newspapers in the East had painted him as gallant and brave in contrast to the cautious Carrington who had treated the Sioux with far too much respect.

The whole incident had sickened Hardcastle. He knew that Carrington was a courageous and honourable man who had been used as a scapegoat, and praise for Shafter had gone well over the top. Shafter was embittered and sick and made no secret of the hatred he harboured for those who had inflicted wounds on him. Hardcastle could not abide the man. The members of the board supported the view that Shafter had done little else but dream of vengeance. Furthermore, it was common knowledge that he had been prescribed a sleeping draught to help him endure his pain. While this point was not pursued further, the judge-advocate had carefully placed a seed of suspicion in the minds of the board members.

Next morning Jared Harris was arraigned. Standing before the court he remained motionless while the verdict was read out. He scarcely heard the words. He knew what they were before the officer opened his mouth. 'Private Harris, you have been found guilty on both the charges of desertion and of sleeping on duty.'

The judge-advocate peered over the top of his spectacles and gazed at him severely, his voice coming with gathering power.

'Private Harris, by far the most grievous offence you

committed is that of sleeping while on sentry duty. You may feel that to go to sleep is a trivial and natural thing, something which in no way deserves a death sentence. In peace, there is a graduation of actions, but in war, nothing is trivial. Every deed is significant. In sleeping, you placed the lives of your fellows in jeopardy. It was a cowardly deed. The enemy could easily have descended on the camp and slaughtered your fellows while they rested. They had placed their trust in you. Indeed, the offence you committed is one of the most serious that comes before this court. It gives me no pleasure to inform you that execution by firing squad is the customary and deserved sentence. Private Harris, have you anything to say before I pass sentence?'

Jared sighed deeply. His mouth had gone completely dry. It had been a brave act for Jessie Millard to give evidence in his defence. Her motives, her emotions, were as unpredictable as the wind, but it was clear she had found some strength in her reverend friend. But now Jared knew that death was reaching for him again, and all determination to resist had been sapped from him. His escape from the noose at Virginia City had only brought him additional torment.

He somehow mustered his voice. 'Sir, I have stated the truth as clearly as I can. There is nothing more I can say.'

'Then will you stand while the sentence is imposed.'

He stood up.

'Private Harris,' the judge-advocate announced, 'in view of the unusual circumstances of this case, and in view of the way you have conducted yourself, this court has decided not to impose a death sentence. Instead, you are sentenced to two years' hard labour, after which you will be dishonourably discharged from the army.'

The breath rattled in Jared's throat. He felt giddy. He nodded his acknowledgement to the officers of the board. He was too stunned to speak.

NINETEEN

It was three years and six months later when Jared Harris arrived in Idaho City in search of James Shafter. He had served his sentence of two years' hard labour at the austere US Military Prison in Kansas, and had been subjected to strict, hair-trigger discipline. His fellow prisoners included murderers, rapists, thieves, as well as deserters. Once again, he kept himself to himself, living off the memories of his past. The spectre of James Morgan Shafter haunted him above all else. Why had the man hated him so? It grieved him to think that such hatred had existed against him, and probably still did, growing deeper through the years. Meanwhile, he worked steadily at whatever tasks he was given, whether it was heavy construction work, carpentry, harness or making shoes. He wrote a letter to the Reverend Elliot, Virginia City, hoping it would find him. He felt a tremendous gratitude to the man, for his influence over Jessie Millard had been a major contribution to saving him from the firing-squad. Weeks later he received a reply.

148

My Dear Jared
I am only a humble servant of the Lord. It was
His will that you were saved and it was my
honour to be the instrument of your salvation.
Also, I was privileged to save poor Jessie from the
iniquity into which she had fallen. She is such a
sweet and charming lady and I am most pleased
to say that we have been joined in holy matri-
mony . . .

Jared could not suppress a laugh. He felt happy for
Jessie. Perhaps the stable of a clerical husband would
bring her stability, unbelievable as it seemed.

At long last his time for release came, and he was
given his dishonourable discharge from the army,
together with five dollars to start in civil life.

He returned to Kentucky to find that his father had
died. He tended Annie's grave, sharing quiet hours of
solitude with her sweetness in his mind and a tear in
his eye.

There was now little family wealth for him to
inherit, and he worked at various jobs, taking employ-
ment on farms and plantations – all the while trying to
put his past behind him. But it would not go away.
Nightmares of his experiences plagued him, and
always the shadow of Shafter and his black hatred rose
above all else. Why had the man despised him so . . .
why?

Eventually he could stand the uncertainty no longer,
and he recalled how Jessie Millard had spoken of
Idaho City. He thus embarked on the journey that he
hoped would exorcise the mystery and the hatred from

his life and bring some purpose to his wasted years.

What he did discover was that the hatred James Shafter nurtured for him could only be resolved by the blast of the gun. A gun concealed beneath the blanket of this apparently incapacitated man whose sanity had declined to irretrievable dementia.

The portly Doctor Samuel Lively had just completed a dressing on old Colonel Appleby's knee, seen him out the door and returned to his dispensary. The doctor, who had been a contract surgeon to the army for many years, was pondering on the surgical procedure for excising a carbuncle on the Andersons' twelve-year-old son, when there was a frantic and continuous clanging of his front door bell. Frowning at such a disturbing interruption, he crossed his entrance-hall and opened the door. He was confronted by a highly agitated Ella Shafter, sister of his patient Major James Shafter who had always given him great concern, for he was ill-equipped to treat the vagaries of the human mind.

'My dear, what's. . . ?'

'Doctor . . . something terrible . . . c-come!'

The breathless woman could hardly string two words together.

'What's happened?' he persisted.

But she was unable to speak further, merely beckoning him with her mouth wide.

Trying to retain his own calm, he stepped back into his hall and retrieved the small bag of instruments and medication that he kept in readiness for emergencies. Within seconds he was following Ella as she rushed towards the Shafters' residence.

As they mounted the staircase, the woman managed to stammer out, 'This man came to visit James. I left them together and . . .'

Further words were out of place. The sight that met them as they entered the bedroom where James Shafter had spent so many hours of turmoil both mental and physical, was horrific.

Shafter was sprawled back in his chair, his head a bloody mess, his sightless eyes gazing up at a ceiling still pockmarked with bullet-holes. His revolver lay close to his trailing hand on the carpet. But it was his expression that was so unnerving, for the mouth of his skeletal visage was widened into what was, quite unmistakably, a grin of blissful satisfaction.

Doctor Lively stepped forward, withdrew his stethoscope from his bag, fitted it to his ears and sounded the major's chest, at the same time taking hold of his wrist for evidence of the pulse. Ella again found her tongue, but he motioned her to be quiet while he listened for sounds of life. A moment later he had the stethoscope from his ears and was shaking his head.

'He's gone, my dear,' he said. 'Taken his own life. He must've pressed the barrel of his gun deep into the groove of his scar. The skull was paper thin there. It's incredible how the power of even a blank cartridge can inflict death.' He gave Ella a questioning glance. 'You did replace his bullets with those blanks I brought?'

'Oh, yes, Doctor. Allowing him live ammunition was too dangerous. All those holes in the ceiling. But I thought blank cartridges would be safe.'

He shook his head. 'The gunpowder necessary to provide a realistic blast . . . the percussion . . . well, you can see the damage. I told you at the time, it was only marginally safer.'

Ella was regaining some of her composure, but her eyes were shining with tears. She dabbed at them with her handkerchief, then peered closely at her brother. 'Why is he smiling?' she inquired. 'He looks so happy, even though he is dead.'

Lively turned his attention to the other body. This man, too, had been shot in the head and his blood had oozed on to the carpet. The doctor stooped down, checked the man's pulse and said, 'Ah.' Then he asked, 'Did he give his name?'

Ella struggled to recover her stunned memory. After a moment she said, 'Harris. Something Harris. I cannot remember his first name.'

Lively emitted a satisfied grunt. His surmising was correct. 'Jared Harris,' he explained. 'Your brother mentioned his name to me many times. James was consumed with a lust to avenge his injuries. That's why he died a happy man. He had nothing else to live for. His mind would have crumbled away. He wouldn't have lasted long, so he had no hesitation at taking his own life, particularly now that he thought he had completed what he had longed to do for years. He viewed it as his duty.'

'Duty?' she queried.

'Yes.' He gently examined the wound in the head of the man sprawled before him. To Ella's amazement, the man was showing signs of life, emitting a groan. 'It's not a deep wound,' the doctor continued. 'Although the gun was fired at point blank range, he must have been at sufficient distance to avoid its most lethal affect. It just gave his brains a good shake up, I guess. But, my dear lady, I suspect that your brother had no doubt in his mind. He believed he had shot dead this man. He died a satisfied man.'

Ella nodded, speechless.

Doctor Lively went on: 'I will get the undertaker to come and take your brother away, and I must get some assistance, so that this other fellow can be carried over to my surgery and restored to normality. Then, he can face any justice that may await him.'

When Jared's confused senses filtered back to him, he was aware of a throbbing headache, and reaching up discovered that there was a bandage around his head. He tried to recall what had happened. He remembered entering Shafter's bedroom, and kneeling down to humour the sick man. Shafter had spoken the words, *'Your execution!'*, cast his blanket aside, a fiendish look in his eyes as he had raised the revolver. After that . . . nothing.

Jared wondered why he was still alive. He had no answer. He realized he was lying on a bed. His eyes drifted around the room he was in. Fancy wallpaper, pictures on the wall, a polished dresser. Thin curtains drawn, admitting sunlight as they were caught in the breeze and billowed back. A fly buzzed around his head. He fanned it away with his right hand. He moved his neck, turning his head from side to side.

He tried to move his left hand and could not. He realized that he was manacled to the bedstead. He groaned. He recalled that he had been manacled previously – so many times. He thought he had left all that behind.

Suddenly he tensed. The door of the room was opening and a portly man with a mop of white hair came in, the floor boards creaking beneath his weight. There was a stethoscope hanging about his neck. He was accompanied by another man, wizened, skinny as a stovepipe, mean looking, his limp moustache drooping over his mouth.

There was a star pinned to his chest.

'So this is the fella Shafter claimed ruined his life,' the lawman remarked. Jared felt his stare settle on him. His eyes were as cold as a lizard's.

The other man, obviously a doctor, was nodding his white head. He met Jared's eye. 'Captain Jared Harris, formerly of Eighth Kentucky Volunteers, I understand.'

Jared did not respond. He resented being chained up.

'I guess you know how you turned Shafter's head,' Doctor Lively went on. 'He spent months pacing around his room imagining he was fighting Indians. But he wanted more than Indians to kill, Mr Harris. He wanted you.'

'Why?' Jared demanded, his anger rising.

'You know well enough,' the sheriff cut in. 'You know well enough what you did to him at Shiloh.'

Jared's mouth sagged. 'I never saw him until he arrived at Fort Phil Kearny.'

Doctor Lively emitted a scornful laugh. 'You saw him at Shiloh, when you shot him down and kicked his head and back in while he lay wounded. He swore blind it was the captain of the Eighth Kentucky.'

Jared was shaking his head in bewilderment. 'I did no such thing.'

'But you *were* the captain of the Eighth Kentucky Volunteers, you can't deny that?'

'Yes, I was,' Jared agreed. And then something clicked into his cobbled mind. 'But not at Shiloh. I was promoted after the battle to take the place of Captain Selby. He was killed during the battle. He sure hated the guts of every Yankee. He . . .'

The doctor and lawman exchanged glances. 'You weren't promoted until after the battle?' the sheriff asked. 'Then why did Shafter swear blind that it was you, Harris, that did the kicking?'

'I guess he put two and two together when he found out I was a Galvanized Yankee and had been captain of the Eighth Kentucky. Put two and two together and arrived at five.' Jared thought for a moment, then added, 'And when I deserted, the belief grew in his twisted mind. Must've became obsessed with the idea of getting even with me.'

'Why should we believe you?' the sheriff asked.

'You only have to check the findings of my court martial at Fort Laramie.' And then, raising his voice defiantly: 'Alternatively you could accept my word as a Southern gentleman!'

The doctor and the sheriff remained silent, taken aback by his outburst.

After a moment, Jared said, 'Can't understand why Shafter's aim was so poor at that range.'

Doctor Lively briefly explained how the gun had been loaded with blanks. Jared shook his head in disbelief. 'Well, let's hope that the entire matter can be laid to rest, and I can get on with leading a normal life again. That is, if you will unlock this damned handcuff.'

Lively hesitated, then he nodded to the sheriff. The latter produced a key from his pocket and soon Jared was freed, massaging his wrist and rising unsteadily to his feet. He felt downright dizzy, but he suspected that given time he would recover.

That evening he was well enough to visit Ella Shafter and express his condolences. She was still in a state of shock at the death of her brother, but she invited him in and they sat in the parlour of the house and talked at length about events that had led up to the tragedy. She even apologized for the mistake her brother had made in branding Jared as the man who had ruined his life. Jared knew that but for the grace of God it could have been himself who had shot down Shafter at Shiloh, but he knew that he would never have descended to the extreme of kicking an apparently dying man as he lay helpless on the ground.

Now, thankfully, the war was over, though the outcome had not been to Jared's liking. But at least some of the old bitternesses, the old ghosts, had been put to rest. As he bade farewell to Ella, leaving her to her grieving, he wished her well. She said she would have James buried with his hat on and a gun in his hand, and his heroism in the Indian wars would be inscribed on a gravestone for all to see.

She asked Jared to write to her, which he said he would. He stayed at a hotel that night and left Idaho City by stage next morning. His mind was made up. He would return to Kentucky. He had been granted the gift of survival, against the most incredible odds. On no account would he squander that gift. He did not know what lay ahead, but he was determined to create some purpose to his life. That was what Annie would have wanted.